T4-AHF-135

# New Critical Essays on James Agee and Walker Evans

PS
3501
G35 Z79
2010
WEB

# New Critical Essays on James Agee and Walker Evans

## Perspectives on *Let Us Now Praise Famous Men*

Edited by
*Caroline Blinder*

## palgrave
macmillan

NEW CRITICAL ESSAYS ON JAMES AGEE AND WALKER EVANS
Copyright © Caroline Blinder, 2010.

All rights reserved.

The editor and publisher gratefully acknowledge permission for use of the following material:
*Let Us Now Praise Famous Men* by James Agee and Walker Evans.
Copyright 1941 by James Agee and Walker Evans; copyright renewed 1969 by Mia Fritsch Agee and Walker Evans. Reprinted by permission of Houghton, Mifflin Company. All Rights Reserved.

The Walker Evans Archives at The Library of Congress, Prints and Photographs Division, FSA-OWI Collection.

The James Agee Archives at the Harry Ransom Humanities Research Center, The University of Texas at Austin.

First published in 2010 by
PALGRAVE MACMILLAN®
in the United States—a division of St. Martin's Press LLC,
175 Fifth Avenue, New York, NY 10010.

Where this book is distributed in the UK, Europe and the rest of the world, this is by Palgrave Macmillan, a division of Macmillan Publishers Limited, registered in England, company number 785998, of Houndmills, Basingstoke, Hampshire RG21 6XS.

Palgrave Macmillan is the global academic imprint of the above companies and has companies and representatives throughout the world.

Palgrave® and Macmillan® are registered trademarks in the United States, the United Kingdom, Europe and other countries.

ISBN: 978–0–230–10292–7

Library of Congress Cataloging-in-Publication Data

New critical essays on James Agee and Walker Evans : perspectives on Let us now praise famous men / edited by Caroline Blinder.
        p. cm.
        ISBN 978–0–230–10292–7
        1. Agee, James, 1909–1955. 2. Evans, Walker, 1903–1975. 3. Agee, James, 1909–1955. Let us now praise famous men. 4. Artistic collaboration—United States. I. Blinder, Caroline, 1967–

PS3501.G35Z79 2010
818'.5209—dc22                                                    2010001852

A catalogue record of the book is available from the British Library.

Design by Newgen Imaging Systems (P) Ltd., Chennai, India.

First edition: August 2010

10  9  8  7  6  5  4  3  2  1

Printed in the United States of America.

*For one who sets himself to look at all earnestly, at all in purpose toward truth, into the eyes of a human life: what is it he there beholds that so freezes and abashes his ambitious heart?*

*For Mamita*

# CONTENTS

# Illustrations

# Acknowledgments

From the University of Tennessee, Knoxville, I must thank Hugh Davis, Mike Lofaro, and Nick Wyman for their expertise, encouragement, and help in accessing the James Agee Archives. To the contributors and participants in the one day conference on *Let Us Now Praise Famous Men*, I also owe a great deal of thanks for making it an extraordinarily inspiring day.

I would also like to thank both colleagues and students at Goldsmiths, University of London for listening to me garble on about Agee with patience and kindness.

And last but not least I would like to thank both Kim and Natasha, the latter who is still hoping I will write a real book some day.

C.B.

# INTRODUCTION

## Caroline Blinder

> My main hope is to state the central subject and my ignorance from the start, and to manage to indicate that no one can afford to treat any human subject more glibly or to act on any less would-be central basis: well, there's no use trying to talk about it. If I could make it what it ought to be made I would not be human.[1]

In the summer of 1936 the writer James Agee and the photographer Walker Evans were sent to Alabama on an assignment by *Fortune* magazine. The aim was to gather material for an article on cotton tenancy or as Agee put it, "a sharecropper family (daily and yearly life): and also a study of Farm economics in the South."[2] When Agee and Evans returned with an unwieldy and extensive set of notes, comments, and photographic material and submitted a forty-page article, *Fortune* promptly rejected the piece.

Five years later Houghton Mifflin finally published what we now know as *Let Us Now Praise Famous Men*. The 500-page book, although reasonably received in critical terms, sold just more than 1,000 copies. Compared with earlier documentary work on rural America such as Margaret Bourke White and Erskine Caldwell's *You Have Seen Their Faces* (1937) and the phototextual collaboration between Dorothea Lange and Paul Taylor *American Exodus* (1939), *Let Us Now Praise Famous Men* (abbreviated as *Famous Men* onward) stood out as much more modernist exercise in how to combine images with writing. The photographs preceded the text, they were uncaptioned and less obviously illustrative and the writing, intensely lyrical, discursive, and philosophical, dispensed with any apparent sociological rigor. In other words, the book was definitely not a straightforward "study of farm economics in the South."

To add to its problematic nature in both written and photographic terms, the timing of the book's publication was less than fortuitous. *Famous Men* originated in the midst of the Depression and yet came out when the encroaching forces of Fascism overseas had turned American politics from domestic issues and toward national patriotism. By the 1940s most picture magazines, *Fortune* included, were using human-interest stories on American industry, economics, and business as a way to provide an optimistic outlook on the U.S. economy rather than criticize centuries of agricultural mismanagement in the South.

Initially given a more suitably neutral title: *Cotton Tenants: Three Families*, Agee's later title *Let Us Now Praise Famous Men* (a quote from Ecclesiastics), deliberately distances the project from its original journalistic aims. The title does several things of course, it positions itself within an existing trope of the 1930s in which titles with religious subtexts, Lange's *American Exodus* (1939), John Steinbeck's *The Grapes of Wrath* (1938), and Zora Neale Hurston *Their Eyes Were Watching God* (1937) to name a few, all played on the mythic and Diaspora dimensions of the Depression. By placing itself within this lineage of narratives of displacement, *Famous Men* could be read as another treatise on the tragic and epic nature of the Depression, a sense augmented by its critique of an American faith in a progressive Capitalism and its simultaneous and lyrical exposition of its rural tradition.

If *Famous Men* appeared to align itself to a tradition of socially conscious and creative responses to the Depression rather than to *Fortune's* idea of journalistic objectivity, it was likewise an effort to write beyond and above much of the proletarian fiction and reportage of the era. Agee was all too aware of the risk of *Famous Men* being caught in a particular type of redemptive rhetoric and was keen to avoid the charge of populist sentimentalism disguised as yet another version of liberal journalism. Agee's unease was thus part of a larger and more encompassing idea, namely how to unite a moral, ideologically sound perspective within a documentary premise. Or, as Agee put it himself in the prologue to *Famous Men*, how "to deal with the subject not as journalists, sociologists, politicians, entertainers, humanitarians, priests, or artists, but seriously" (xv).

Above all, according to Agee, one could not and should not take "an undefended and appallingly damaged group of human beings, an ignorant and helpless rural family, for the purpose of parading the nakedness, disadvantage and humiliation of these lives before another group of human beings" (*FM, 7*). This fact was not lost on contemporary critics such as Alfred Kazin for whom *Famous Men* was not only "written to end all documentary books...it has special importance...because it is an unusually sensitive document and a work of great moral intensity...it represents a revolt against the automatism of the documentary school...an attack on the facile mechanics and passivity of most documentary assignments."[3]

Kazin was writing on *Famous Men* in his seminal *On Native Grounds* (1945), a book which sought to trace how the American literary voice was shaped by and in turn shaped national and artistic concerns. Similarly, Lionel Trilling's Kenyon Review from 1942, "Greatness with One Fault in It," linked Agee's more experimental prose with a distinctly moral and to some extent political agenda. For Trilling the ornate descriptions of the sharecroppers, rather than alienating the reader, allowed a convergence between the individual artistry of Agee and Evans and the collective plight of the sharecroppers.[4] For these early critics, Agee's style was more akin to high modernists such as William Faulkner and John Dos Passos than to ethnographic and/or sociological scholarship per se.

Since then, accepting Agee into a canon of high modernism, if this is indeed the aim, has proven less straightforward.

Not only have the parameters of what constitutes American modernism shifted, but the integration of a so-called documentary voice and what it might mean has proven equally hard to define. Following the resurgence of interest in *Famous Men* in the 1960s and its popularity among a radicalised student body with an interest in documentary sociology, William Stott's *Documentary Expression and 1930s America* (1973), Maren Stange's *Symbols of Ideal Life—Social Documentary Photography in America 1890–1950* (1989), and Robert Coles's *Doing Documentary Work* (1997) considered the documentary aspects of *Famous Men* as symptomatic of both a distinct set of aesthetic and narrative devices and, on a wider level, a particular 1930s zeitgeist.[5] For Stott, Agee's tendency to be "exuberant, angry, tender, wilful to the point of perversity" whilst also "romantic and even sentimentalizing" did not detract from *Famous Men*'s documentary qualities, it merely proved that a documentary perspective lay within the intersection between the private and the public and that it was all the more powerful for it.[6]

In line with such readings, the book's curious mixture of sociology, lyrical prose, modernist anguish, politics, and ethnography, rather than symptomatic of the failure of documentary practice has since oftentimes been seen an example of its zenith in artistic terms. According to Keith Williams in "Post/Modern Documentary: Orwell, Agee and the New Reportage (1997): "questions about reality, truth, subjectivity and language raised by modernist writing…swarm back toward, and are even welcomed into, Agee's text.…The debate about realism was for Agee par excellence the point at which politics and poetics become indivisible."[7]

Williams's reading of Agee as somehow acknowledging the limitations of both modernism and documentary practice, is symptomatic, to some degree, of what happened to readings of *Famous Men* as its enthusiastic entry into documentary studies abated. Thus, during the last decades, *Famous Men*'s mixture of documentary purpose and literary and visual experimentation has made the book "readable" from so many angles that it paradoxically has cancelled out its inclusion into many English and American literature departments. Nevertheless, as several chapters indicate here, readings of *Famous Men* as leaning against a postmodern as much as a modernist aesthetic also have their problems. As Allan Trachtenberg points out, there is the possibility that the combination of Agee's writing with Evans's photographs is genuinely symptomatic of a 1930s desire "not so much for change as for 'recovery', a return to basic values, to fundamental Americanism."[8] On a purely emotive level, the sombre black and white portraits of the Gudger family, the interiors of the sharecroppers' homes with their Spartan preindustrial furniture and bare wooden walls lean toward this type of "Americanism." This partly explains why these photographs have become such natural iconic images of the 1930s. Another reason for this lies in the fact that Evans's uncaptioned photos tend to appear more accessible compared to Agee's 500-page text with its constant authorial intrusions and commentary. In reality, as several chapters indicate in this collection, Evans's images are as multilayered and complex in narrative terms as the text that follows them. Questions arise, then, as to whether Evans's ascendancy in the 1970s as the photographer of 1930s Americana would have happened regardless of or indeed was boosted by the text in *Famous Men*. Perhaps, as Mark Durdon suggests in "The Limits of Modernism: Walker Evans and Agee's *Let Us Now Praise Famous Men*" (2002): "it is possible that Agee's reflexive, engaged, and impassioned writing alerts us to the limits of Evans's Modernism rather than vice versa."[9]

Despite various attempts to situate *Famous Men* within a modernist and/or postmodernist paradigm, the fact that it cannot easily be defined as one or the other continues to be a mainstay of Agee criticism. When *Remembering Agee*, a seminal collection of reminiscences, commentaries, and critical examinations emerged in 1972, the essays on Agee's reputation as a film critic, poet, and prose writer combined a highly biographical and historical approach with more critical readings of individual works.[10] Writers and friends of Agee, Dwight

McDowell and Robert Fitzgerald spoke of their memories of Agee as an inspirational force in creative terms but above all, of his larger-than-life personality, thus solidifying an already growing cult of Agee.

Although the chapters in this edition aim primarily for close readings of *FM*, the issue of "a cult of Agee" is countered and taken into account in different ways. Agee's insistence on writing as defined by its limitations, as well as accomplishments, could be seen as a blueprint for the book overall. In similar terms, the chapters here all acknowledge the difficulty in providing any *one* reading of a writer notoriously difficult to pin down. They also share a mutual delight in the dialectical process of establishing rather than answering questions. Thus the chapters here look closely at the texts themselves as both enabled and handicapped by the respective personas of the artists and how other issues impact on this. In this respect, the recent publication of more archival material has proven invaluable in looking at how Agee actually pieced together some of his more intricate writing. What procedures and mechanisms, in other words, can we distinguish as distinctly Ageeite without necessarily taking his personal history into account?

The aim of these critical chapters is to provide a measure of the book's complicated status at the beginning of the twenty-first century as much as establish exactly what field to position the book in; an aim, one must suppose, which would have heartened Agee. Rather than circumvent the intersections between American modernist writing and other disciplines such as photography, sociology, ethnography, and cinema, to name a few, Agee wholeheartedly embraced them. The strength and genuine challenge of writing about *Famous Men* lies precisely in how to deal with these intersections. Agee—after all—lamented his inability to genuinely reflect the circumstances of his subjects' lives and yet insisted on conveying "his immeasurable weight of actual existence," the fact that the sharecroppers—just as himself—existed "as human beings" (*FM*, 12).

Philosophically speaking, Agee's promise to convey the "immeasurable" aspects of the sharecroppers' existence is, of course, impossible, and this is accentuated by the numerous admonitions, retractions, and contradictions, by, from, and indeed within Agee. There are few other writers from the 1930s who ask so much from their readers (apart perhaps from that other enfant terrible Henry Miller). What can only be read as a tendency to conceptualize in abstract terms is often underpinned by a convoluted literary and—in the true sense of the word—sanctimonious style. According to Jeanne Follansbee Quinn in "The Work of Art: Irony and Identification in *Let Us Now Praise Famous Men*," "Agee actually uses the Christian sacrament of communion as a structuring metaphor...and a solemnization of his affinity with the Gudgers."[11]

This apparent religiosity, while a way to discern a pattern in what may otherwise appear very unstructured, springs from what Alan Spiegel argues is Agee's desire to illuminate an already unified and coherent set of concerns and obsessions. Focusing on Agee not as "a poet, a critic, a novelist, a screenwriter, a journalist...but as a consistently unified writer," Spiegel—in his 1998 *James Agee and the Legend of Himself*—sees Agee as a writer for whom "the same images and obsessions evolved in continuity from book to book."[12] For Spiegel, Agee's attraction to larger moral issues is as deep rooted as his attraction to a more shambolic form of anarchical modernism.

Complicating matters is the issue of what editorial moves Agee undertook, if any, to make *Famous Men* more consistent and how this relates to the photographs preceding the text. Evans's stature as the patrician figure of American vernacular photography tends to mask the possibility that he too may have embarked on the project with a sense of artistic trepidation. Despite the fact that Evans appears to have had no significant qualms about the selection of his photographs for the first edition, he included a larger amount when *Famous Men* was reprinted in 1960 after Agee's death. In this respect, the anxieties of collaboration and the mechanisms implicit in trying to unite the textual and the visual need to be addressed. Similarly, there is a great deal still to be said of the ways in which the book is symptomatic of, and indeed straddles, the anxieties of two decades both politically and aesthetically. In similar ways, the completion of the book, because it took so long, inevitably straddled the ascent as well as descent of Agee and Evans's lives as artists with their own idiosyncrasies and problems over a considerable stretch of time.

In this context, Henry Luce, the managing editor of *Fortune* has to be credited with allowing the paring of Agee and Evans in the first place. Agee and Evans knew of each other but without the financial support of *Fortune* they would not have been able to execute the necessary fieldwork. Strangely enough, while it is commonly acknowledged that Evans's photos are an instrumental part of *Famous Men*, Evans—as coauthor— still remains a somewhat shadowy figure. Even stranger, it is often as though the astonishing clarity of Evans's photographic vision of the sharecroppers somehow cancels out his own presence on the other side of the camera. One of the problems, which several of the chapters here seek to rectify, is the tendency to deal with Evans's photographs as separate from Agee's text, as though the photographs are in a league of their own and thus "untouchable" from critical scrutiny. Nevertheless, considering the tangible/actual results of the collaborative process between Agee and Evans does not necessarily make a plea for commonality in fact it may acknowledge its impossibility.[13]

Such thinking does not, however, preclude an analysis of Agee and Evans's shared interest in providing a working definition of vernacular American culture, or more to the point, how it manifests itself in aesthetic terms. How does one render a quintessential American experience? Is there such a thing in the first place? At the same time, Evans and Agee's interest in European models of the avant-garde, the unconscious, the psychoanalytical, the anarchical are all continental models of thought, which often resist rather than embrace the idea of a vernacular truth. How does *Famous Men*, for example, incorporate Whitmanesque as well as Surrealist imagery? How does it move from the vernacular to the classical, from the contemporaneous to the timeless without diluting its subject, the actual lives of the sharecroppers in the process?

Despite protestations to the contrary, Agee as well as Evans were acutely aware of their respective statuses as international and not just American artists. In this sense, the issue of how *they* wanted to be remembered was as crucial as how they wanted the sharecroppers remembered. Who exactly the famous men are in *Let Us Now Praise Famous Men* remains, as many have noted, far from obvious. The deliberate irony of the book's title lends itself toward a personal form of mythologizing not to mention the importance *Famous Men* places on the idea of the self in general. Part of the attraction surrounding Agee's persona as the artist tormented by his father's accidental death when he was a little boy cannot be ignored in this respect; Agee's overall oeuvre seems so insistently about absent father figures and on a wider level about death and how it relates to life. Circling around the idea of the self in *Famous Men* is the idea of an unavoidable absence as well, not just the absence of shelter and sustenance and how the self deals with it, but the absence of love and empathy and genuine understanding.

For Mick Gidley, the tenuous line between self and other is indeed a very serious strategy in *Famous Men*. Taking as his starting point the line from Ecclesiastics, Gidley sees the "praise" of famous men as partly an elegy for the dead. Memorialization, or rather, the attempt to convey what Gidley calls a "strategy of multiple address," in which Agee speaks to both us and the sharecroppers as part of a decidedly self-reflexive literary gesture, is likewise partly promulgated on the book's inevitable proximity to death. In "Ontological Aspects of *Let Us Now Praise Famous Men*" the quote from Ecclesiastics, on a wider level, connects the issue of commemoration and utterance by establishing itself as an ongoing process and proof in a sense that Agee intends to keep the narrative open-ended. As Gidley points out, early criticism of the book acknowledged its unclassifiable and subversive aspects as exceptional qualities, qualities designed to destabilize stereotypical representations of the sharecroppers and

Southern poverty. If *Famous Men* is marked by the problematic of representation, in terms of both in terms of its generic
format and the difficulties of doing the sharecroppers justice,
it is also a book, which through utterance is still being written
and revised. This is not dissimilar, Gidley argues, to the ways
in which Evans's photographs still elicit widely differing readings as well. In this respect, *Famous Men* is doing exactly what
Agee wanted it to do; namely accentuate through the actual
writing the tenuous line between self and other, between life
and death. As in William Faulkner's *As I Lay Dying*, which
Gidley uses by way of comparison, the presence of death in
*Famous Men* ensures, paradoxically, a form of communality, a
hub for a particular but necessary utterance. Rather than read
death as an ending or void, death becomes an invitation to
remember the living, and the proximity of death allows Agee
the opportunity to commune with us—the readers—and the
sharecroppers equally.

The importance of and problems surrounding communication also lie at the heart of John Dorst's ethnographically
inspired reading of *Famous Men*. In "On the Porch and in the
Room: Threshold Moments and Other Ethnographic Tropes
in *Let Us Now Praise Famous Men*," the infamous house of the
Gudger family, and in particular the porch where the family
is photographed, is set up as another threshold between life
and death and between the perspective of the outsiders—in
this instance Agee and Evans—and the insiders, the occupants
of the house. Dorst extends this reading by metaphorically
linking the house with Evans's camera eye and Agee's ethnographic gaze, visual metaphors, which both in different ways
invite the possibility of an "unblinking" examination of the
sharecroppers. Of course, no such thing genuinely exists and
indeed the camera lens, in this instance, can do no more than
stress the play between interiority and exteriority, between
going inside and becoming part of the family or remaining
tentatively on the porch. Although this could be seen as a
quintessential ethnographic trope, *Famous Men* is nevertheless remarkably full of these "threshold moments"; moments

where the subject/object divide collapses in the face of Agee's mixed feelings regarding his relationship to the family and to the project overall. Agee both wants to enter the interior space of the families investigated and yet recognizes that an element of transgression is inevitable in this process, but, as Dorst points out, this is also part of the book's strength. The book is both bound by the unspoken contractual agreement between the investigators and the investigated and determined to break that contract.

The seemingly insurmountable chasm between the culture of the sharecroppers and the "investigators" is never downplayed; rather, it accentuates the ethical implications of cultural identity. The camera, for example, is set up as a device for surreptitious examination but also allows a safety net between the Gudgers and Agee. Like the porch, the lens in this instance becomes the threshold across which exterior reality is pulled into interior space, a movement that is equally mimicked in Agee's desire to get us, the readers, to enter the house and by implication the text with him.

Using the camera as a starting point for a rereading of *Famous Men*, Alan Trachtenberg reenters and interrogates this territory, albeit from a different perspective, through an examination of Evans's photographs in "Walker Evans's Contrapuntal Design: The Sequences of Photographs in the First and Second Editions of *Let Us Now Praise Famous Men*." Seeing Evans as a "photographer of revelations," Trachtenberg queries whether the heart of Evans's aesthetic lies not so much in a straight-forward documentary ethos but rather in the comingling of historical facts with a form of poetic intervention. This comingling is not only unique to *Famous Men* but also a distinctive part of Evans's overall oeuvre. In thinking about the South as an idea both constructed and envisaged rather than just a regional entity, Trachtenberg argues that the attraction of Hale Country Alabama lay not merely in its emblematic destitution and economic collapse, but in its applicability as a site wherein the twin sensibilities of Evans and Agee could have free reign. Thus a form of pastoralism, albeit

configured in distinctly modernist terms, has to be taken into
account and not just as an "Ageean" trope in keeping with his
romanticism but as something contained within Evans's work
as well. In this respect, Evans's so-called look of objectivity,
as Gidley also points out, is in reality a far more complex and
oftentimes oblique mechanism. If Evans came to the South
with a particular "cosmopolitan sensibility," it was one that
had to reconstitute itself faced with the demands of a Southern
ethos, regardless of whether it was found or constructed. As
Trachtenberg points out, Evans may in fact have desired an
affiliation with a certain Southern tradition; a renewed sense
that regional affiliation could be more than just emblematic
of a local vernacular culture. The issue, as in Dorst's examination of territory in ethnographic terms, is what happens when
a sense of "reciprocity between place and consciousness" leads
to a concurrent sense of both participation and detachment.
By tracing some of the changes in the sequencing and structure of Evans's photographs in the first and second editions
of *Famous Men*, Trachtenberg points out that the narrative
implicit in the photographs is often one of searching for an
identity. As such the characters in *Famous Men* can be seen as
redemptive figures, not merely for Agee and Evans's artistic
sensibilities but for a bruised nation looking toward a pastoral
past as well.

In Sue Currell's "The Tyranny of Words in the Economy
of Abundance," the issue of representation in *Famous Men*
can indeed be traced back to a bruised nation. Looking more
closely at the fascination with linguistics in the 1920s and 30s,
an interest made all the more urgent because of a general culture of political anxiety and a sense that language on a wider
level was loosing its meaning, Agee, Currell argues, was caught
up in this desire to define the exact function of words. As a
student at Harvard, Agee was influenced by contemporary linguistic theories concerning the ethical implications of language
and it was this interest that Agee took with him in later writing. Clearly it was crucial for Agee, Currell points out, to test
the limits of language and democracy in literary terms without

falling into a modernist form of solipsism. Looking back to Pound's aesthetic considerations around logopoeia, among other things, Agee is seen to engage in the period's interest in the rhythmic and the visual as radical literary gestures in their own right. Keeping in mind that the initial remit for *Famous Men* was for publication in *Fortune* magazine, Currell points out that the lyricism of *Famous Men* is in stark contrast with the language of advertising and the increasingly commodified language of contemporary journalism. If the headings in advertisements ironically parallel Agee's listings and descriptions in *Famous Men* of clothing and kitchen utensils, among other things, they also contrast a corporate consumerist vision of the United States with the actual abject poverty of the sharecroppers. In this respect, Currell sees Agee's writing as operating within a landscape of modernity, but it is a modernity increasingly infiltrated by commercialism as well as an untenable desire for a form of writing purified and transparent in linguistic terms. The desire to speak directly without contamination from outside interests attests, in other words, to the importance placed by Agee on the very idea of communication as an essential component of writing.

Currell's point, that Agee was dramatizing how a decline in language could be linked to a decline in society, takes an interesting twist in Paul Hansom's polemical argument in "Agee, Evans and the Therapeutic Document: Narrative Neurosis in the Function of Art." For Hansom, language always inscribes and tries to circumscribe the neurosis which he claims lies at the heart of the creative process. In doing so, Agee and Evans are engaged in a "working out" of such neurosis despite the promise of political and social concern for the sharecroppers. Although this manifests itself in different ways for Agee and Evans, for Hansom, *Famous Men* constitutes a complex and necessarily incomplete exercise in writing "the self," a book in which anxieties about existence, death, and effacement are at the heart of the creative process. Indeed, modernity for Hansom spurs this process along, as it appears to provide artists with a tenuous promise of permanence through and with their art. Above all, Hansom argues, *Famous Men* reflects this desire by insisting throughout on a self-reflexivity where the visual and the verbal are designed to establish the presence of the artist. Moving Agee from the proverbial porch as the threshold place where the internal and the external meet, where both Agee and Evans position themselves seemingly at a vantage point, Hansom instead places Agee on the analyst's couch. Haunted by myths of transparency and objectivity within the documentary process, Agee utilizes the farmers literally and figuratively as a pretext for an exploration of his own psyche. For Hansom, this is about auto-history rather than social history, with the sharecroppers curiously incidental to Agee's musings about his own consciousness. Although Hansom moves Agee from the vantage point of the porch, it remains a central metaphor of a place where the collision between the external and the internal, the familiar and the uncanny, as Hansom puts it, is symptomatic of many of the digressions and contradictions in the book overall.

The issue of belonging, retraced in different ways by Gidley, Trachtenberg, Currell, and Hansom, circles around the basic question of what it means for an investigator/writer to participate and remain subjective at the same time. Thus, for example, while Hansom sees Evans as shrewdly engaged in promoting himself as a modernist artist/genius, this, paradoxically, both counters and compliments Trachtenberg's version of Evans as a man who wanted to "belong" in the South. Evans considered photography, just as many other poetic interventions of the period, as a genuinely transformative and transcendent art form. Although Hansom sees Evans's images of the sharecroppers as an exercise in divorcing them from their social and economic context by turning them into aesthetic objects first and foremost, Trachtenberg sees Evans's refashioning of the sequence of southern photographs as proving the opposite, namely that Evans wanted the families inserted into an actual wider regional and social context.

If the porch constitutes one of the quintessential and largely necessary threshold moments in *Famous Men*, a suitable

location for the "analyst's couch," Paula Rabinowitz chooses
the colon as, among other things, another threshold.  In
"Colon," Agee's inserted section Rabinowitz argues that the
grammatical definition can be extended to indicate a quintessential aspect of Agee's writing. In "Two Prickes: The Colon as
Practice" Rabinowitz makes the case for Agee's writing as not
only performative but also a performance staged both inter-
nally in psychological terms and externally through a variety
of textual mechanisms. In this respect, the colon becomes a
description of a methodology in which the extension, the supplement, the long sentence, signals—once again—anxieties
about closure and ultimately death. Thus the colon is both a
sign of punctuation and a sign of continuation, it indicates, as
Rabinowitz puts it, that the writing is "complete but needing
a supplement." In a Derridian sense, the colon/supplement
is both theme and system, it indicates an incompleteness and
absence and therefore partly explains Agee's disrespect for lin-
ear writing. This foregrounding of the use of radical punctuation has—as Rabinowitz points out—a long and venerable
history within American literature. Like Whitman and Hart
Crane, Agee not only foregrounds the components of speech
but ties in ideas of the index and of simultaneity as a sign of
sacredness, of writing as circular and never ending, with his
perspective on the farmers. In essence the colon is much more
than an inserted section or an aside, it functions, even though
seemingly divorced from political content, as a most radical
literary gesture in its own right.

     Gesturing, or rather moving, toward a reading of *Famous
Men* in terms of ritual and communion reappears in my own
contribution " 'Animating the Gudgers': On the Problems of a
Cinematic Aesthetic in *Let Us Now Praise Famous Men*." Here,
the issue of how photography and cinematography converge in
*Famous Men* illuminates, among other things, how Agee com-
municates what he considers the sacred nature of the Gudgers.
Keeping Agee in mind as a writer attuned to the visual on
multiple levels, I try to question the more common reading of
Agee as spell bound, to some extent, by Evans's expertise as a

photographer. For Agee, photography could be seen more as a means toward an end in this instance, the desire to memorialize the Gudgers and at the same time prove the immeasurable weight of their "actual existence." Such tactics are nevertheless complicated by the ways in which the more descriptive passages within the text operate vis-à-vis the photographic material. What happens when Agee's process of visualisation deliberately aims for a sense of flux as opposed to the more static and contemplative stance of Evans? Is it possible, at all, to distinguish a photographic and/or cinematic language in Agee's writing in the first place? The concept of animation as something that provides at least the possibility of a spiritual rebirth for the Gudger family becomes a crucial denominator here and to some extent the prerequisite for a significantly religious aspect of Agee's sensibility. Striking a precarious balance between stillness and movement, between life and death in the Gudger home, Agee's writing is partly a constant battle to keep the subjects alive and simultaneously memorialize them. This process, I argue, takes place in a tenuous space between cinema and photography, between the desire to keep the Gudgers alive through movement and fix them forever through photography.

Like Hansom and Rabinowitz, I see Agee's use of particular rhetorical devices as somehow beyond contemporary aesthetic theories concerning language and the visual, as though the book as an object deliberately situates itself between an impossible sociological premise and an equally impossible narrative one. The way in which communality is about a great deal more than the successful ability to communicate with people across social, political, and economic divides exemplifies this to some extent. Linking the interior life of the artist with his or her external subject, in this case "the South" with all of its psychological and regional connotations, becomes a way to question the very foundations of documentary work. If Agee and Evans utilized preexisting ideas of what the South should be in the 1930s, as Trachtenberg argues, they did so to question the responses of a Northern "liberal" audience and to establish that the South still harboured certain ideals such as loyalty and steadfastness. In this context, the regionalism in *Famous Men* necessarily struggles between familiarity and strangeness, between a sense of connectedness and the fear of exile. Agee himself continuously expresses his personal desire to belong with the sharecroppers as well as the realization that he never really can.

The ties between a regional and personal sense of connectedness is in many ways a constant driving force behind *Famous Men*. Not dissimilar to other phototextual projects from the period, the farmers in *Famous Men* can be seen as redemptive figures for a nation desperate to confirm its agrarian and pastoral dreams during the hardships of the Depression. For Agee and Evans the issue is how to turn this desire for redemption inward in personal and artistic terms as well. The insertion of additional photographs of the South in the 1960s edition, as mentioned previously, seems to indicate a desire on Evans's behalf to insert the sharecroppers into a wider social context as well as to make the book reflect his own photographic interests.

In the end, Evans and Agee's collaboration was always based on the desire to produce a body of work, which they themselves felt had integrity, rather than a successful *Fortune* article. As William Stott points out in his epilogue, we have enough documentation in terms of correspondence and manuscripts to get a strong sense of the symbiotic nature of the professional as well as personal relationship of Agee and Evans. Although it may appear obvious that Evans, in some ways, was a father figure to Agee, Agee also needed Evans on a more professional level. Stott surmises that Evans's editorial hand may have had a larger role in putting together *Famous Men* than we think, a book, which after all was more or less continuously revised for more than four years. Whether Evans's later input in the 1960 version made the book less "Agee-ish" and more of an exercise in documentary aesthetics, as Stott indicates, is worth considering. Stott's theory adds to Trachtenberg's insistence that Evans's emotional involvement in the book should not be underestimated. It is possible, for example, that Evans's insertion of material in the second edition is a response, not only to changes in the ways in which the South was perceived, but also to certain narrative aspects he felt Agee had overlooked.

Whether Evans was more of a pragmatist in terms of his photographic outlook or chose to present himself as such years after the book's publication and the lamentable death of Agee is a different issue. Their respective personas, regardless of how much we focus on the text itself, remain intrinsically linked to *Famous Men*. It is hard, if not impossible, to not personalise the project, to not make it their child or perhaps more accurately a prodigy extracted under difficult circumstances. Despite its verbose nature the book is, after all, also about desire, joy, and transfiguration in a bodily and metaphysical sense. Are we doing Agee and Evans a disservice by yet again dissecting their progeny or do we accept that most nonacademic of premises that *Famous Men* was above all a labor of love? In the following chapters this is left as an open issue, which is undoubtedly the most honorable thing to do.

## NOTES

1. *Letters of James Agee to Father Flye* (New York: George Braziller, 1962), 105.
2. Ibid., 92.
3. Alfred Kazin, *On Native Grounds: An Interpretation of Modern American Prose Literature* (San Diego: Harvest, 1945), 495.
4. Lionel Trilling, "Greatness with One Fault in It." *Kenyon Review* 4 (1942), 99–102.
5. William Stott, *Documentary Expression and Thirties America* (Chicago: University of Chicago Press, 1973); Maren Stange, *Symbols of Ideal Life* (Cambridge: Cambridge University Press, 1989); Coles, Robert, *Doing Documentary Work* (New York: Oxford University Press, 1997).
6. *Remembering James Agee*, ed. David Madden and Jeffrey J. Folks (Athens: University of Georgia Press, 1997), 110.
7. Keith Williams, "Post/Modern Documentary: Orwell, Agee and the New Reportage" in *Rewriting the Thirties—Modernism*

*and After*, ed. Keith Williams and Steven Matthews (London: Longman, 1997), 173.

8. Alan Trachtenberg, *Reading American Photographs: Images as History Mathew Brady to Walker Evans* (New York: Hill and Wang, 1989), 247.

9. Mark Durdon, "The Limits of Modernism: Walker Evans and James Agee's *Let Us Now Praise Famous Men*" in *Literary Modernism and Photography*, ed. Paul Hansom (London: Praeger, 2002), 29.

10. *Remembering James Agee*, ed. David Madden and Jeffrey J.Folks (Athens: University of Georgia Press, 1997).

11. Jeanne Follansbee Quinn, "The Work of Art: Irony and Identification in *Let Us Now Praise Famous Men*," http://findarticles.com/p/articles/mi_qa3643/is_200107/ai_n8958534

12. Allan Spiegel, *James Agee and the Legend of Himself* (Columbia: University of Missouri Press, 1998), 19.

13. The recent publication of archival material relating to the notebooks, manuscript versions, and tangential material of Agee's in particular, has enabled much more thorough examination of the writing itself. See *James Agee Rediscovered: The Journals of* Let Us Now Praise Famous Men *and Other New Manuscripts*, ed. Michael A. Lofaro and Hugh Davis (Knoxville: University of Tennessee Press, 2005).

# 1

## ONTOLOGICAL ASPECTS OF *LET US NOW PRAISE FAMOUS MEN*: DEATH, IRONY, FAULKNER

*Mick Gidley*

The first words of *Let Us Now Praise Famous Men*, those of the title itself, sound—indeed, resound—a note of irony. We know they are a quotation, an echo from beyond the text, and because they are coupled with what seems at this initial point the book's subtitle, "Three Tenant Families," if we do not recognize their origin we nevertheless feel a friction: baldly, members of tenant families are not famous. For all readers, this is a friction that will chafe until, even after, the still unsourced passage from which they come that is printed toward the very end of the text.[1] For some readers, the irony will be sharper and associated with death.

Erik Wensberg, in a review of the 1960 edition of *Famous Men*, was probably not the first to make a telling analogy when he wrote, "Agee's versatile prose is by turns minutely reportorial, 'magical'...and lyric, stately as legend, and always...at a greater or lesser distance from the bardic, which is its natural mode. One thinks sooner or later of the Bible."[2] Readers familiar with the Bible would think of it *immediately*, well before needing to reckon with the versatility of Agee's prose in any of its modes. In the Bible, among the books of the Apocrypha, the passage of Ecclesiastics inaugurated by the words "Let us now praise famous men" (Ecclesiastics 44.1–14) constitutes, of course, an elegy for certain of the dead. It is apparent there, if not at once, that those spoken of were not all "famous," not all "men renowned for their power" or "such as found out musical tunes, and recited verses in writing;" rather, the rhetorical emphasis is shifted from such known personages onto those who would otherwise "have no memorial," those "who perished"... as though they had never been; and are become as though they had never been born: humble men and women, presumably labourers and artisans, who had furthered life only by the sweat of their brows and the raising of children. That is, the biblical stress—later explicitly carried over into the text of *Famous Men* when the verses of Ecclesiastics are reproduced as a freestanding section just before the book's "Notes and Appendices"—duly falls, tongue in cheek, on the forgotten rather than on the famous.

While the verses of Ecclesiastics constitute an elegy (all those memorialized are already dead), as they ring out, the elegist's primary concern becomes not so much to release those spoken of from the annihilation of death itself as to rescue them from the lack of recognition they had experienced in life. Here, as in the cliché of death as the great leveller, the powerful (those "honoured in their generations") and the powerless (those "which have no memorial") not only go down together, but they also rise together in communal commemoration: "Their bodies are buried in peace; but their name liveth for evermore." And their names live *in and through* the very utterance of the elegist. Not surprisingly, these issues raised by the title reverberate through, and beyond the text.

Poet and novelist Harvey Breit, one of the earliest reviewers of *Famous Men*—and one of the most perceptive—made the then startling claim that it is "a heterogeneous book. It is an appeal for a continuous *tension* and it is propaganda intended to corrode our habitual acceptances. It is a book about Mr. Agee. It is a book that refuses to call itself a book." And, he implies, it is not really a book.[3] Breit was probably echoing a passage in *Famous Men* by Agee himself—since much quoted—to the effect that, if it were possible, he would be providing not written text but "fragments of cloth, bits of cotton, lumps of earth, records of speech, pieces of wood and iron, phials of odours, plates of food and of excrement" (*FM*, 13), or another in which, Whitman-like ("he who reads this touches a man"), Agee insists that *Famous Men* "is a *book* only by necessity" (xi; italics in original). There is much evidence for the relevance of such a view.

In keeping with a subsidiary aim of this chapter to acknowledge more than is often the case the insights of some of the early commentators on *Famous Men* and its project, I wish to draw attention to Alan Holder's 1966 essay "Encounter in Alabama: Agee and the Tenant Farmer." In it, Holder shows, with contrasting examples, that an urgent impetus for *Famous Men* was the necessity to counter the prevalent 1930s stereotype of the sharecropper as shiftless, primitive, innately inferior, yet inevitably necessary to the natural social order. Holder argues that *Famous Men* attempted to counter this image not just in its "content," but also in its "format" as what he terms an "anti-book." He provides an excellent succinct description of the text's eccentric front matter and the "Notes and Appendices," and then says, "What Agee seemed to be trying was to keep his reader off-balance by the placement, proportioning, and miscellaneousness of his prefatory and appendix materials, doing his best to prevent *Famous Men* from being 'only a book,' from being even in its physical form what his reader presumably expected to find on opening it." Holder terms this strategy an aspect of Agee's "hostility" to the reader. And, for the bulk of the essay, Holder examines Agee's expressions of "guilt" over the tenants' condition and his inability to do anything about it, claiming that Agee's distress with himself and his hostility to the reader are the corollary of his sense of the "beauty" and profound innocence of the tenants.[4]

*Famous Men* is certainly an excessive text, and as early as 1948 Agee's friend Dwight Macdonald emphasized the multiplicity of kinds of discourse in its verbal portion, likening it in this respect to Melville's *Moby Dick*. In 1957, W. M. Frohock found it unclassifiable, asserting that Agee "lacked, even more than other writers of our time, the traditional respect for genres." Several commentators since Holder, Macdonald, and Frohock have pointed to these and other features that make it exceptional: its large scale; the inclusion of the unintroduced, untitled, and uncaptioned Evans photographs as, we later realize, "Book One;" the range of kinds of writing within it; the complexity of its structure and layout; and its very marked self-reflexivity at every level, from its repeated signposting of its own structure to its musings about the problematics of representation, as in such footnotes as: "The whole problem, if I were trying fully to embody the house, would be to tell of it exactly in its ordinary terms" (*FM*, 134).[5]

It is also, as a text, unstable in a variety of ways:

- famously begun as a journalistic magazine assignment—and part published as such—it became a book that, in turn, claimed to be only the first installment of a larger three-volume publication, a project never completed, and possibly not even undertaken;
- the parts of the text that appeared in periodicals ahead of its book appearance were not entirely the same as they were to be in the finished text;
- the number and the identity of the photographs within it were not fixed but, with Evans' active involvement, changed from edition to edition—and, with the cooperation of the Evans Estate, have continued to do so in the most recent editions.[6]

In fact, it would be profitable to consider *Famous Men* not only as extraordinary but also as *different in kind*, as a phenomenon that overlaps with but exceeds the text itself.

Interestingly, in his full and searching study of the project's photographs, William Stott argues that what he calls "*the* classic photograph of *Let Us Now Praise Famous Men*"—a picture of the Gudger family at ease with itself, in which George Gudger "needs no one's pity" as "the master of the brood" able to relish "his fortune" as such—is not actually *in* any edition of the book. Implicitly, for Stott the project is more than the actual text of *Famous Men*. And if we continue to think primarily of the photographs for a moment, artist William Christenberry's work carries the story onward, past the death of Agee, through Evans's later visit to Hale County, in which the homes of the tenants featured in *Famous Men* were situated, through Evans's death, into Christenberry's own childhood and later memories of the (now properly named) tenant families, and right on into his own photographic and sculptural depictions of their houses, local stores, and landscapes.[7] And just as the text of *Famous Men*—prose as much as pictures—seems to overflow the covers of the book; the project has no certain terminus.

Ahead of everything else in *Famous Men*—at least in the original edition, and in the better editions since–is an Evans photograph. Before any of Agee's verbal text, with all its hesitations, false starts, and self-reflexive strategies comes the first photograph of the sequence—or, at least, series—that constitutes Evans's contribution to the text. From the initial reviews onward, there has been a tendency to regard Evans's work as separable from Agee's, as in some way different to Agee's, even as in opposition to Agee's, and sometimes this binary approach has resulted in the formulation that if Agee's text is difficult, intractable, and self-absorbed, then Evans's photographs are direct, transparent, relatively "straight" (in the photographic sense of the term), and permit immediate access to their subjects. Ralph Thompson's review in the *New York Times* is typical of those initial reactions that saw the verbal aspect of the book as (in his words about Agee) "arrogant, mannered, precious, gross," while discovering revelation in Evans's pictures: "There never was a better argument for photography." Similarly, a few years later, the sociologist C. Wright Mills, while admiring aspects of Agee's method—which he rightly identifies as a species of "participant observation" akin to those of the social sciences—had a complaint: "Agee often gets in the way of what he would show you, and sometimes...there is only Agee and nothing else." On the other hand, Mills sees Evans's pictures as "wonderful because the cameraman never intrudes in the slightest way upon the scene…The subjects of the photographs…are just there, in a completely barefaced manner, in all their dignity of being, with their very nature shining through."[8]

But let us look at that first image. Given its premier position in the text, the surprise is that most commentators have ignored it, and only a few have tarried over any aspect of it. Some remark, at best, that it depicts the landlord of one of the tenants and notes his crumpled jacket. Even Stott, despite his

**Figure 1.1**   Walker Evans, "Landowner in Moundville, Alabama" 1936

*Source:* Courtesy of Library of Congress, Prints and Photographs Division, FSA-OWI Collection [Reproduction number: LC-USF342-008127-A].

concern for detail, comments only on the status of the landlord (named Chester Boles in the text of *Famous Men*) as "middle class" and on his "determined mask," his capacity for "successful deception," implying that his class membership is readable from the photograph, and that it necessarily grants him a disguise unavailable to the (inevitably lower-class) tenants whose images—as vulnerable, damaged, open,—are to follow. Such an interpretation makes us, of course, register the landlord— even if as a person he is not seen as individually powerful (or perhaps *because* he is not seen as individually powerful)—as representative of the pervasive and shaping determination of market forces in the lives of the tenant families.[9]

Other readings, however, are possible. First, insofar as the images are sequenced, it may be that because in the narrative of the text to follow we meet the landlord before we meet the tenants, so in the "narrative" comprised by the images we dutifully encounter his picture ahead of theirs. Second, if the landlord has donned a mask, how is this intimated *visually*? It is *not* as if he is depicted as one of "the lords of the land" (to use the Left vocabulary of the time adopted and adapted by Richard Wright in his directly contemporary photo-text *12 Million Black Voices*), nor are his stature and status augmented by being seen (from slightly below) *as* a master, in the manner, for example, of Dorothea Lange's "Plantation owner, Clarksdale, Mississippi, June 1936."[10] Rather, he is presented, or presents himself—despite the social markers of his tie and his jacket (which *is* assuredly rumpled and hardly a sign of blinding affluence)—as frontally as any of the tenants. His eyes, it is true, are ever so less discernible than the eyes of some of the tenants when they are captured from a similar distance, but he does seem to be looking directly at the camera. It is hard to read him as deceptive or, even, evasive. Almost everything about him, in fact, is a kind of declaration, down to the wedding ring that shines on his left hand. He stands with his arms beside him, simply hanging rather than folded over his slight potbelly in the manner that the just visible folds and creases of his jacket seem to indicate his more usual posture.

Any subterfuge, if such there were, would have to lurk in the suggestion of a smile on his face and this mostly because we habitually associate pictured smiles with mystery. Any subterfuge, in other words, would be apparent only to someone well acquainted with him who could say, "This is not the man I know."

Now, I would argue that Evans's images of the tenants, too, are less open or "barefaced," to use Mills' word, than much commentary assumes. (Even Stott—while declaring the portraits "stubbornly enigmatic"—sees their subjects as "wholly exposed.") The next image in the series—the famous portrait of the top half of George Gudger [Floyd Burroughs] in his overalls, the darkness of the doorway around his head, his eyes looking at the camera or "beyond" it, unsmiling, perhaps troubled—is a case in point. In comparison with the representation of the landlord, it is a more visually complex image, but it is not its greater complexity that accounts for its difference. Rather, it is that through it the person being depicted makes an almost uncanny claim upon our attention. We are aware of a human presence that is precisely *not* "wholly exposed." Again, one of the initial book reviews might provide some insight. Speaking principally of the third image in the series, of Annie Mae Gudger [Allie Mae Burroughs], cultural critic and novelist Lionel Trilling, in describing beautifully how Evans's photograph allows her to "defend herself against the lens," rightly observes: "The gaze of the woman returning our gaze checks our pity ... In this picture, Mrs. Gudger ... simply refuses to be an object of your 'social consciousness'; she refuses to be an object at all—everything in the picture proclaims her to be all subject."[11] Mr. and Mrs. Gudger, each is "all subject."

Some of this potent presence and appeal are attributable to Evans—to his artistry and technical skill—and perhaps also to the much-vaunted mechanized "realism" of the medium of photography itself. Breit, in his early review, suggests an appropriate balance: he rejects the power of the photograph as that of mere transcription, going for something subtler: "Here there is, by the very nature of the medium, a more possible identification. The shutter has no prejudices. But when Mr. Evans brings you face to face with the woman who is biting her hand there is an impulse to reject Mr. Agee's belief that the camera's function is 'to perceive the cruel radiance of what is.' " As Breit perceives the situation, "there is a fine and complicated sensibility at work in that photograph."[12] I would agree, but, as in the less-insistent case of the landlord, our awareness of the subjectivity of Floyd and Allie Mae Burroughs is also attributable to the Burroughs themselves and, where it is manifest in their portraits, to the other tenants. They gave themselves so fully to the camera (if not necessarily to its operative)—that is, to the *photograph*—that when we look at their images now, their presence makes a claim upon us. As Stott and other critics have said, Evans's subjects, as we see them in *Famous Men*, compose themselves for the camera. Possibly, they even perform for the camera, but not *only* for the camera: they are also themselves, for themselves. Yet, ontologically, this is a paradox: as Roland Barthes claims in his discussion of what it means "to see oneself" in a snapshot, "the photograph is the advent of myself as other."[13] In Evans's powerful images, self and other are not entirely separate and fixed categories. As we shall see, Agee's prose also encourages us to realize this.

T. V. Reed, deploying parallels to post-structuralist ideas of "text," points out the differences between *Famous Men* as a "putatively self-sufficient artefact" and what I am referring to as "the project" around and beyond it, a project "caught," as Reed puts it, "in a web of intertextual and extratextual relations." According to *Famous Men* itself, a strand of that web is made from "Detail of gesture, landscape, costume, air, action, mystery, and incident *throughout the writings of William Faulkner*" (*FM*, 397, emphasis added). Partly prompted by Alfred Kazin's observation, made as early as 1942, that *Famous Men* emulates "the deep personal suffering of Faulkner's novels," I want to suggest certain parallels with one of Faulkner's major representations of poor white life in the South: *As I Lay Dying* (1930).[14]

Although the Bundrens of Faulkner's novel appear to own their land rather than rent it as sharecroppers, they are indigent and, it seems, often dependent on others. Just as Agee's subjects, the Bundren family is very fully realized. We witness, through their diverse eyes, the sparse furnishings of their tilted house, the physical labor of the cotton field, the precise carpentry of one of the sons, the loading of a wagon, and numerous further features of subsistence living. The crucial point is that the Bundrens are represented principally not in material terms but in existential—even religious—ones. Darl undergoes a continuous crisis of identity, always lying "beneath rain on a strange roof," thinking of "home" even when he is, actually, at home (Faulkner, *As I Lay Dying*, 76); Addie's brief section recounts her attempts to define herself and fairly brims with paradoxical musings on the nature of being (*As I Lay Dying*, 161–68); simple Dewey Dell has experienced moments when she lost a sense of herself: "*I had a nightmare...I thought I was awake but I couldn't see and couldn't feel...and I couldn't think what I was I couldn't think of my name I couldn't even think I am a girl I couldn't even think I*" (*As I Lay Dying*, 115); and even Anse, despite his immense physical and mental laziness, indulges in half-nutty reflections on man being made "up-and-down ways" and thus unfitted for roads made "long ways" (*As I Lay Dying*, 35), for all the world as if in absurd parody of certain renaissance ideas on uprightness as a sign of the divine nature of human kind.[15]

As conveyed by the novel's curious title, primary rites of passage for the self or "I"—from "emptying" oneself "for sleep" (*As I Lay Dying*, 76), through sex, to death—are both paramount events and topics of discourse. The words of the novel's title, as others have noted, would in "reality" be syntactically nonsensical or unsayable, in that they would have to be uttered *from* death. It is only in mythological or religious discourse—or, of course, in fiction—that such things can be said. Fundamentally, in *As I Lay Dying* apparent binary opposites—humor/horror, sanity/insanity, activity/stillness, sleeping/waking—are called into question. I now want to

suggest, if too briefly, as in *Famous Men*, the chief such categories questioned are the most elemental ones of self/other
and life/death.

Addie's section, in which, among much else, she also speaks
of her husband as "already dead" when he is still alive, is placed
in the action of the novel after her death, as if she might be
speaking or thinking beyond the grave. And in annotating her
death, the doctor, Peabody, reflects, "I remember how when I
was young I believed death to be a phenomenon of the body;
now I know it to be merely a function of the mind and that of
the minds of those who suffer the bereavement." "The nihil-
ists," he continues, "say it is the end; the fundamentalists the
beginning; when in reality it is no more than a single tenant or
family moving out of a tenement or a town" (*As I Lay Dying*,
42–43). Seen in this way, a death or rather death itself (which
we usually associate with aloneness, and ultimately with being
forgotten) becomes a collective experience, a social event.
Paradoxically, in death a person could be more remembered
(and more a member of society) than he or she had been in
life. The fact that a person, however simple, exists, qualifies in
some manner the existence of every other person with whom
he or she comes into "contact," and even others more remote.
Thus, from person to person, an endless "series" could cover
the earth. No wonder that Addie declares, "how terribly doing
goes along the earth" (*As I Lay Dying*, 165). Addie likens herself to a circle, excluding so much and excluded from so much,
but she is ultimately wrong, as is Darl when he thinks of her
as the rim of a wheel (*As I Lay Dying*, 102). The opposite is
finally true: she is like each individual human being, a hub
from which the spokes radiate.

The metaphorical and associative chain of sleep, sex, and
death recurs, and to similar effect, in the verbal dimension to
*Famous Men*. It is also there, so to speak, if in an obviously
more muted and necessarily more exterior way, in the photographs. It is not an accident, for example, that the image that
succeeds the two portraits of the Gudgers presents their marriage bed, or that the child Squinchy Gudger is shown covered

and so deeply asleep—and, of course, so still—that he could
be shrouded in death, or that the penultimate image is of a
child's grave. And, of course, as well as the notion, already
mentioned and attributed to Barthes, that the photograph
may point up a dissociation between the self (as interiorized
by the self) and the self "out there" for others to see, there is a
long-standing, naturalized connection between photography
and death, from Emerson's sense that the freezing of his face
for the camera was a premonition of death, through so-called
primitive beliefs about photography as theft of the soul, to—as
in *Famous Men* itself, in the cemetery description—the use of
photographs of loved ones on graves (*FM*, 436).

There are numerous points in the verbal portion of *Famous
Men* that connect sleep, sex, and death. For example, late in the
narrative order of the text, Agee offers a detailed and somewhat
amusing description of trying, as a guest, to sleep in a bed full
of bugs, aware that they are endangering his health and life,
of killing them, and of attempting "to imagine intercourse" in
the bed he couldn't get to sleep in ("I managed to imagine it
fairly well," he quips [*FM*, 374–77]). A key link in the sleep/
sex/death chain is the famous passage in which Agee evokes
rather than describes the Gudger family asleep in the adjoining
room (*FM*, 51–52), and so fully that he imagines himself joining them, more than metaphorically, in sleep: "I become not
my own shape and weight and self, but that of each of them,
the whole of it, sunken in sleep like stones; so that I know
almost the dreams they will not remember, and the soul and
body of each of these seven" (*FM*, 52). His descriptions take
in the intimate parts of their bodies and, during the following
pages, which are partly a kind of aftereffect of this reverie and
partly a continuation of it, he speculates on George's sexual
feelings for his sister-in-law Emma, and hers for him; and he
even wonders about the possibility of Emma desiring to go to
bed, perhaps simultaneously, with George, Walker Evans, and
himself! (*FM*, 55).

In what plotwise might be a continuation of the reverie,
Agee later registers the dawn waking and breakfast routines

of the Gudgers and members of the other families on the hill, the Ricketts [Tingles] and the Woods [Fields] (*FM*, 78–81), presenting some of this activity as if he is seeing it *from* their varied viewpoints. Eugene Chesnick, in one of the earliest essays to question the "realism" of *Famous Men*, found a "kinship of sensibility" between Agee and Whitman. He noted the affinities between Agee's identification with the sleeping family and the similar identification in Whitman's extraordinary poem "The Sleepers," with its erotic aspects and its linkage of sleep, death, and time's renewal.[16] But more than just Agee's "sensibility" is involved and at stake here.

Frequently the text overtly tackles ontological matters. Sometimes such matters nudge out from the mundane, as when, in a disquisition on the doors of wooden houses, the description ends with death: "a special odour, very dry and edged: it is somewhere between the odour of very old newsprint and of a Victorian bedroom in which, after a long illness, and many medicines, someone has died and the room has been fumigated, yet the odour of dark brown medicines, dry-bodied sickness, and staring death, still is strong in the stained wallpaper and in the mattress" (*FM*, 136). At other times, the ontological concerns fully announce themselves, so to speak: "how it can be that a stone, a plant, a star can take on the burden of being" (*FM*, 51); or "I lie where I lay this dawn. / If I were not here; and am alien; a bodyless eye; this would never have existence in human perception" (*FM*, 164). (This last line could almost be a quotation from *As I Lay Dying*.) All told, while it is entirely appropriate that the text venerates the camera as "the central instrument of our time," it is even more important to note the precise emphasis with which this reverence is granted: "the camera seems to me, next to unassisted and weaponless consciousness, the central instrument of our time" (*FM*, 9). I take "unassisted and weaponless consciousness" to mean the capacity both to be and to reflect upon being. Thus conceived, "unassisted and weaponless consciousness" is the supreme attribute of the human being, however lowly.

In comparison with *As I Lay Dying*, the element "added" by
*Famous Men* is the sense of social elevation as a consequence
of "the effort," as the text puts it, "to recognize a portion of
unimagined existence, and to contrive techniques proper to its
recording, communication, analysis, and defence" (*FM*, x). In
having their "existence" fully "imagined," the lowly tenants
*are*, in a sense, ultimately "famous." In the graveyard scene
near the end of the book, after detailed descriptions of the
burial plots, especially of the children, Agee—in an echo of
Ecclesiastics and presaging the words of the Lord's Prayer that
conclude the chapter—suddenly addresses a particular dead
child and, as he proceeds, he seems also to address the tenants
and/or the reader and/or, even, God: "I dread to dare that I
shall ever look into your eyes again: and soon, quite soon now,
in two years, in five, in forty, it will be all over, and one by one
we shall all be drawn into the planet beside one another; let us
then hope better of our children, and of our children's children; let us know...there is an end to it, whose beginnings are
long begun" (*FM*, 386–87).

Interestingly, in a late Faulkner text *The Mansion* (1961),
Mink Snopes, one of Faulkner's poorest of poor whites,
someone whose life is fated by a combination of his economic
circumstances and the machinations of a rich and predatory
kinsman, knowingly achieves in death a comparable elevation while, paradoxically, moving earthward: he feels himself
pulled down, "beginning to creep, seep, flow easy as sleeping...following all the little grass blades and tiny roots,"
but "free now," with "the folks themselves...all mixed and
jumbled up comfortable...so wouldn't nobody even know or
care who was which any more, himself among them, equal
to any, good as any, brave as any, being inextricable from,
anonymous with all of them: the beautiful, the splendid, the
proud and the brave, right on up to the very top...among
the shining phantoms and dreams which are the milestones
of the long human recording—Helen and the bishops, the
kings and the unhomed angels, the scornful and graceless
seraphim."[17]

We have noted the marked reflexivity of the text of *Famous Men*, which necessarily swings some of the focus away from the book's ostensible subjects, the tenant farmers, and places it on Agee: his ideas, doubts and convictions, his desires (including even his sexual daydreams about one or another of the tenant women), and, of course, his aspirations for the text in the making. And, as we know, the text's photographs, in a different way, are likewise reflexive. This double reflexivity also shifts the focus onto the reader.

Sometimes the shift is strikingly overt, especially in the written text, as when Agee addresses the reader as "you." Chesnick, in considering what he calls "the difference between the fictional and non-fictional performance," notes a switch in Agee's use of "you" in the text, sometimes to address (one of) the tenants themselves, sometimes to address the "sophisticated reader" or readers: "The poor whites are the ones Agee wants to understand him, but they are miserably equipped to deal with his prose. A necessary audience alternates with a preferred audience."[18] In addition, to say "you" is sometimes really to say "I," as in, "You may or may not waken some dogs [as you go down the path]: if you do, you will hardly help but be frightened" (*FM*, 67). Indeed, in *Famous Men* "I," "you," "he," "they" are frequently interfused. As we have witnessed, in this text death is and is not final, the self does and does not end where the other begins. What we encounter is a sort of boundaryless consciousness. I would claim that much of the verbal portion of the text amounts to an extended rhapsody of consciousness itself. Ultimately, *Famous Men* is *about* consciousness, being, and selfhood, their fluidity and mystery, and—just as in the elegy from Ecclesiastics—the utterance itself is the means by which recognition for the forgotten may be achieved.

The text's intimation of the larger project around it calls for an unusually active imaginative response. The sense of *presence* of the tenant family members, especially in the photographs, beckons us beyond the realm of representation. The verbal text's reflexivity, ironies, allusiveness, and the strategy of multiple address demand a special attentiveness. In fact, in one passage, *Famous Men* directly, if somewhat contortedly, seeks "cooperation" from the reader: "All this,…you can see, it so intensely surrounds and takes meaning from a certain centre which we shall be unable to keep steadily before your eyes, that should be written, should be listed,…as if all in one sentence…and I shall not be able so to sustain it, so to sustain its intensity toward this centre human life,…it is this which so paralyzes me: yet one can write only one word at a time,…and if they [the words] sink,…then bear in mind at least my wish, and…restore them what strength you can of yourself" (*FM*, 97–98). Such expressions amount, at the very least, to a plea that we *acknowledge* what is always implicitly the situation in any reading and/or viewing experience, that we complete the text, we determine its vibrancy and meaning. With *Famous Men*, we might well be hesitant: it is a heavy responsibility. If not quite literally, there are selves to be realized and lives at stake.

## NOTES

1. *Let Us Now Praise Famous Men* ([1941] Boston: Houghton Mifflin, 2001), title pages and, for the unattributed verses from Ecclesiastics, 391–93. All subsequent references are to this edition and are located within the text.
2. Erik Wensberg, "Celebration, Adoration, Wonder" [rev. of *Famous Men*], *The Nation* (Nov. 26, 1960), 417–18; quotation, 418.
3. Harvey Breit, "Cotton Tenantry" [rev. of *Praise*], *The New Republic* (Sept. 15, 1941), 348–49; quotation, 348. Breit's extremely perceptive comments are of the sort that would be developed later by, e.g., T.V. Reed (see n5 below).
4. Alan Holder, "Encounter in Alabama: Agee and the Tenant Farmer," *Virginia Quarterly Review* 42 (Spring 1966), 189–206. On the other hand, Holder seems to believe too easily that the camera provides unmediated access to reality itself and quotes Agee on photography to the same effect: "all of consciousness is shifted from the imagined, the revisive, to the effort to perceive simply the cruel radiance of what is;" at the same time,

however, he sees Agee's endeavor as an elaborate verbal effort to get beyond the period's usual "documentary pattern, in which the pictures were the dominant feature" (Holder, 194–95).

5. Dwight Macdonald, "After Seven Years: 1. A Way of Death" in *Politics* 5 (Spring 1948), 123–25. W. M. Frohock, "James Agee, or The Question of Wasted Talent," in *The Novel of Violence in America* (London: Arthur Barker, 1959), 212–30; quotation, 218; essay first published in *Southwest Review* 42 (Summer 1957), 221–29. For relevant readings of *Famous Men*, see (in chronological order) Eugene Chesnick, "The Plot against Fiction: *Let Us Now Praise Famous Men*," *Southern Literary Journal* 4:1 (1971), 48–67; William Stott, *Documentary Expression and Thirties America* (1973; Chicago and London: University of Chicago Press, 1986), 261–314, especially 290–314; and T.V. Reed, "Unimagined Existence and the Fiction of the Real: Postmodern Realism in *Let Us Now Praise Famous Men*," *Representations* No. 24 (Fall 1988), 156–76. By contrast, Victor A. Kramer is probably the most convincing of those critics who see the achievement of the book as a triumphant *realism*, an extraordinarily full and vivid representation of tenant farming; he readily acknowledges the deployment of a range of rhetorical strategies, the insistence of Agee's own subjectivity, and the construction of what he terms "levels of realism," but resists any suggestion that rhetoric or subjectivity might cut across or delimit the text's realism; typical of this stance is his "Agee's *Let Us Now Praise Famous Men*: Image of Tenant Life," *Mississippi Quarterly* 25:4 (Fall 1972), 405–17.

6. Points abstracted from data provided in commentaries cited in note 5. Material on Evans's development of the photographic sequences may be found in Alan Trachtenberg's contribution to the present book.

7. Stott, *Documentary Expression*, 284–87; quotation, 286, italics added, and Stott also reproduces "the classic" image as his penultimate illustration. For examples of Christenberry's work, see Thomas W. Southall, *Of Time and Place: Walker Evans and William Christenberry* (Albuquerque: University of New Mexico Press in association with The Friends of Photography and the Amon Carter Museum, 1990), a book that includes Christenberry's reminiscences of both the tenant families and Evans. Subsequent references to the tenants will indicate both Agee's aliases for them and their actual names.

8. Ralph Thompson, "Books of the Times" [rev. of *Famous Men*], *New York Times* (Aug. 19, 1941), 19. See C. Wright Mills's note "After Seven Years: 2. 'Sociological Poetry'" in *Politics* 5 (Spring 1948), 125–26. It should be said that other critics have almost ritualistically looked for similarities between the verbal and visual elements; e.g., Wensberg found Agee's prose "in its own way, photographic" (p. 417); and Miles Orvell's juxtaposition in his *The Real Thing: Imitation and Authenticity in American Culture, 1880–1940* (Chapel Hill and London: University of North Carolina Press, 1989) 273–85, especially 278–84.

9. Stott, *Documentary Expression*, 267–89; quotations, 275. Susan Hegeman, in an interesting wider discussion of *Famous Men* as both the supreme (anti-) documentary of the 1930s and the inaugural modernist work of liberalism in the cold war period, offers the useful suggestion that to Stott, and perhaps to Evans and Agee, the landlord is *necessarily* deceptive precisely because, by contrast, it had become a trope of 1930s documentary that "the rural poor are by definition the subject matter of honest imagery" see her *Patterns for America: Modernism and the Concept of Culture* (Princeton, NJ: Princeton University Press, 1999), 158–92; quotation, 180.

10. Richard Wright, with photo direction by Edward Rosskam, *12 Million Black Voices* (1941; New York: Thunder's Mouth Press, 2002). Lange's photograph is reproduced, among other places, in Wright, *12 Million*, 30, where it is neither titled nor dated.

11. Stott, *Documentary Expression*, 274. Lionel Trilling, "Greatness with One Fault in It" [rev. of *Praise*], *Kenyon Review*, 4 (Winter 1942), 99–102 [100–101].

12. Breit, "Cotton Tenantry," 350. Stuart Kidd's *Farm Security Administration Photography, the Rural South, and the Dynamics of Image-Making, 1935-1943* (Lewiston, NY and Lampeter: Edwin Mellen Press, 2004) provides a larger frame and, in the course of it, presents Mr. Gudger [Burroughs] image as the result of *cooperation* between Evans and his subject (*LUNPFM*, 132–33).

13. Roland Barthes, *Camera Lucida*, trans. Richard Howard (London: Cape, 1981), 12.

14. Reed, "Unimagined Existence," p. 176, n16. Reed invokes Barthes's repeated distinction between "the work" and "the

text," which becomes for me the distinction between "the text" and "the project." William Faulkner, *As I Lay Dying* (New York: Vintage, 1964); subsequent page references are given parenthetically in the text. Alfred Kazin's comment is taken from his *On Native Grounds: An Interpretation of Modern American Prose Literature* (New York: Reynal and Hitchcock, 1942), 495, n1.

15. See C. A. Patrides, "Renaissance Ideas on Man's Upright Form," *Journal of the History of Ideas* 19 (1958), 256–58. For more on Faulkner, especially the ontological themes of *As I Lay Dying*, see Mick Gidley, "Beyond 'Beyond': Aspects of Faulkner's Representation of Death" in Lothar Hönnighausen, ed., *Faulkner's Discourse* (Tübingen: Max Niemeyer, 1989), 223–33.

16. Chesnick, "The Plot against Fiction," 61. For an illuminating discussion of "The Sleepers," see Alan Trachtenberg, "Whitman at Night: 'The Sleepers' in 1856," *Yale Review* 94:2 (April 2006), 1–15.

17. William Faulkner, *The Mansion* (London: Chatto and Windus Collected Edition, 1965), 399.

18. Chesnick, "The Plot against Fiction," 49 and 51.

## 2

# ON THE PORCH AND IN THE ROOM: THRESHOLD MOMENTS AND OTHER ETHNOGRAPHIC TROPES IN *LET US NOW PRAISE FAMOUS MEN*

*John Dorst*

It hardly needs repeating that the deceptively straightforward photographs that open *Let Us Now Praise Famous Men* constitute one of Walker Evans's masterpieces; a classical monument built from minute textures and quotidian subtleties. Among these subtleties is a motif that appears often enough to qualify as a full-blown theme. We might call it the "ambiguous point of entry." His treatment of architectural openings in the *Famous Men* photographs—porches, doors, hallways, hearths—amply illustrates Evans's famous deployment of shadow as a compositional element. In a number of the images darkness obscures a point of entry, usually in stark contrast to the sharply defined façade it pierces. For example, the hard-edged, asymmetrical funnel of shadow in the doorway of a rural schoolhouse (plate 57) both draws our gaze and prevents its entry (see also, plates 5, 9, 13, 16, 39, 51, 52, 59).[1] This image is a particularly direct expression of the visual theme I am talking about here: the emphatic marking of access points and simultaneous denial, or at least complication, of entry.

I take this visual trope in Evans's photographs as my own entry point for an examination of a rhetorical location James Agee occupies repeatedly in his documentary masterpiece. Often poised ambivalently at points of entry, obsessively attempting to resolve the irreducible dilemma of the documentarist's identity, Agee anatomizes one of the core conventions of modernist ethnography. Scenes of arrival or first contact, of introduction, of recognition, and so on, are among the tropes that have come to define the genre of narrative ethnography, both in its popular documentary forms and in academic social science as well. As with so many aspects of *Famous Men*, this persistent attention to entry scenes, and I include those occasions of failure to gain access, seems prescient.[2] The mode of "reflexive" ethnography that emergences some thirty years after *Famous Men* virtually requires close scrutiny of how the fieldworker "gets in" to the field site.[3] The process of gaining access is where the ethics of documentary work are most clearly at issue. It is in his unrelenting self-examination, if not self-flagellation, over the moral implications of presuming to enter the damaged lives of three tenant farm families that Agee anticipates the reflexive turn in ethnographic writing.

In what follows I will mainly be viewing *Famous Men* in the context of these ethnographic practices rather than in terms of documentary journalism. The book's relation to the latter, so brilliantly interpreted by William Stott in his indispensable *Documentary Expression in Thirties America* (1973), may be taken for granted. Less obvious perhaps, and certainly less commented on, are the ways other direct observation or "field based" modes of writing resonate in the Agee/Evans classic.[4] The literary landscape of twentieth-century nonfiction is immensely complicated, of course, and its genre boundaries have been more fluid than with fiction, at least until the wholesale disruptions of postmodernism. It is especially in its "threshold moments" that *Famous Men* overlaps with forms of writing more likely to be shelved under social science than as journalism.[5] These are the places where Agee develops, however unsystematically, virtually an axiology of entry, and in

doing so scoops the ethical circumspection of reflexive ethnography by several decades.[6] The threshold is an especially
apt metaphor for the textual moments I am talking about
here, because the architecture of the vernacular house is one
of the two master symbols through which Agee prosecutes his
unblinking self-examination.

The other is the camera. In poetically enjoining Evans to
use the photographic apparatus ("sharpen and calibrate") to
"order the façade of the listless summer" (*FM*, 4), Agee metaphorically connects the house and the camera. I will be elabo-
rating this connection in terms of the play between exteriority
and interiority that the architectural threshold and the camera
lens both signify. Before turning to these artifacts, though,
I will try to sharpen my own focus by considering the three
rather odd vignettes in the "July 1936" section of *Famous Men*.
Each is a threshold moment of some sort, and collectively they
echo the variable ethnographic trope of the "arrival scene,"
itself a rhetorical device that long predates the emergence of
professional ethnographic writing in the twentieth century.

Comparative literature scholar Mary Louise Pratt has shown
how the "scientific" discourse of academic ethnography partakes, despite its early pretensions to clinical objectivity, of literary patterns from more subjective nonfiction genres. The
dramatizations of arrival in alien territory or of first contact
with the inhabitants of an exotic culture are commonplaces
of explorers' accounts and other forms of travel narrative.
Ethnography adopted this trope early on and elaborated it
in particular ways. For example, as Pratt demonstrates, some
early ethnographic arrival scenes are painted in utopian pas-
tels, with the white ethnographer surrounded and marveled
over by the welcoming indigenes. This version has a long heritage, especially in the literature of South Seas exploration.[7]

In contrast, and more relevant here, is the type of arrival
scene where difficulties and shocks are the focus of the drama.
Travel adversities, difficult living conditions, indifference on
the part of those one has come to study, and despair over the
seeming impossibility of making meaningful connections

characterize this dystopian version of ethnographic arrival. One famously extreme example of the type is the arrival scene in Napoleon A. Chagnon's monograph *Yanomamö: The Fierce People* (1968):

> The entrance to the village was covered over with brush and dry palm leaves. We pushed them aside to expose the low opening to the village. The excitement of meeting my first Indians was almost unbearable as I duck-waddled through the low passage into the village clearing.
>
> I looked up and gasped when I saw a dozen burly, naked, filthy, hideous men staring at us down the shafts of their drawn arrows! Immense wads of green tobacco were stuck between their lower teeth and lips making them even more hideous, and strands of dark-green slime dripped or hung from their noses (Chagnon, *Yanomamö*, 5).

Although exaggerated to the point of caricature (one almost suspects conscious parody), this image of the ethnographer halted at the threshold by the resistant force of an opaque reality "inside" may serve as a paradigm for the discursive situation in the three documentary vignettes of arrival at the beginning of *Famous Men*. And there is another reason to cite Chagnon in this context. The "we" in the above passage refers to the ethnographer himself and to his "guide," an American missionary who is already known to the people of this village from his five years' work in the area. He has agreed to bring Chagnon to the Indian settlement and provide an introduction. Reliance on a mediator of some sort—classically, missionaries or colonial administrators—to facilitate entrée is common in anthropological fieldwork, though it is often glossed over in early ethnographic texts. That Agee should foreground this figure in the first of his arrival scenes is just one example of how he anticipates the more critical reflexivity of recent ethnographic practice.

Immediately following his first nighttime reflections as he lies on the front porch of the Gudger house ("On the

Porch: 1"), Agee takes us on a rather excruciating sojourn to a small settlement of black sharecroppers. In this first fully narrative episode of the book, "Late Sunday Morning," Agee and Evans set out with Harmon, "a landowner and New Deal executive," and the unnamed landlord of the farmers they will be visiting. One clue that ethnographic conventions might be lurking in the background is this man's response to Evans's request for permission to take photographs. He is told to take as many as he likes, if he "can keep the niggers from running off when they see a camera" (*FM*, 23). It is hard to think of a more familiar ethnographic marker of exotic primitivism than the natives' fear of and/or fascination with the devices of modern technology, the camera above all, perhaps.

When the four men drive up to the cluster of sharecropper houses, a common motif of utopian arrival scenes comes into play. The "natives" start to appear from various directions, as if compelled by some magic force invested in the very bodies of the white visitors. The male residents gather, "as if they had been under some sort of magnetic obligation to approach just this closely and to show themselves" (*FM*, 25). As throughout the book, Agee sweeps the scene with his finely tuned emotional sensors and picks up a range of tones, from the foreman's courtesy as host, to the distanced respectfulness of his visiting relatives, to the quiet but open hostility in the eyes of the women. It is precisely in this sort of nuanced sensitivity to the internal states of others, or to characterize it more abstractly and theoretically, this textual construction of the imagined internalities of inaccessible Others, that Agee transforms received ethnographic and documentary tropes into the tools of a complex aesthetics/ethics.

And we see in this arrival scene another pervasive feature of *Famous Men*, namely, the symbolic correlation between the intangible internalities of emotion, sense impression, and thought and the material internalities of spaces and objects. Agee perceives immediately that his arrival has interrupted activity in spaces he cannot see or enter: the quiet enjoyments of the men "out at the far side of the house" and of the women inside getting dinner. Such subtleties of imaginative perception and metaphoric nuance are well beyond the ken of most ethnographic writing, whether of Agee's day or since.[8]

After these moments of relatively modest discomfort, the episode quickly turns into a harrowing depiction of multiple victimizations. One might go so far as to speculate that Agee puts this particularly painful encounter up front because it is his most graphic example of the inevitability of ethnographic/documentary domination. Furthermore, it shows how he himself is caught up in the role of victimizer, despite his most fervent wishes to the contrary. As the landlord begins to bludgeon everyone with disrespectful vulgarities, we quickly realize that Agee and Evans are the intended and captive audience at a small, self-aggrandizing performance of "easy familiarity" between master and subordinate, coded as manly sexual banter. In a classic colonialist maneuver, the landlord directs his questions at the sharecropper foreman, even though the persons asked about are there at hand. The scene is thick with layers of victimization. The most acute for Agee, no doubt, is finding himself trapped in the role of victimizer—the humiliated—but also unavoidably humiliating spectator at a coerced performance. "In a perversion of self-torture," he confesses, "I played my part through" (*FM*, 28). He could hardly do otherwise.

The close kinship between professional ethnography and the global project of colonialism needs no elaboration at this late date, but it is worth noting that in this episode of *Famous Men* Agee reproduces one of the paradigmatic expressions of this affinity, the colonial administrator's (landlord's) command that the natives (black sharecroppers) present themselves to perform (show "what nigger music is like") for the unknown and anonymous white ethnographers (documentary journalists) who offer payment (fifty cents) and depart when the ordeal is over. Though probably not thought of in these terms, Agee's choice to start with this version of the ethnographic arrival scene, its ethical taint so thoroughly obvious, asserts immediately the ultimate impossibility of gaining full access to the subordinate Other. The other two vignettes, which are perhaps less arrival scenes per se than scenes of "chance first encounter," another ethnographic threshold trope derived from travel literature, highlight different aspects of the moral complexity of Agee's position.

The scene in "At the Forks" shows us the traveling documentarists in search of an acceptable "field site" for their journalistic investigations. Finding the right place—a sufficiently "representative" situation, an identity that makes sense to the documentary subjects, a vantage from which a meaningful range of activity will be visible—is another kind of threshold moment in ethnographic work. The movement toward reflexive ethnography in the 1960s and 1970s commonly took the form of bifurcated accounts, one part constituting the "scientific" record of observed kinship patterns, social organization, means of subsistence, belief and ritual, and so on, the other a personal account of the ethnographer's experiences and interactions. Often this division occurred within the single monograph, with the personal account relegated to an introductory chapter and the bulk of the text devoted to the "real data" of social science. Chagnon's study of the Yanomamö follows this pattern. Alternatively, some anthropologists produced two volumes, one the clinical monograph and the other a reflection on the fieldwork experience.[9] In either form, most of the personal accounts devote considerable space to describing the arduous task of "getting in" and finding the workable location for gathering the data that then shows up in the academic monograph. Often this drama of entrée includes encounters with indigenous mediators or helpers who point the ethnographer in the right direction. In the second of Agee's vignettes he literally has the way pointed out for him by locals, but as in the first episode, this convention becomes the occasion for the compressed introduction of core dilemmas in documentary ethics. As Agee approaches the roadside watchers to ask which fork will be best to follow, he perceives the young couple in aesthetic terms, as having "too much and too outlandish beauty not to be legendary" (*FM*, 30). Indeed, they sit together against the porch wall "as if sculptured [*sic*], one in wood and one in metal" (ibid.).

However, this classical frieze comes apart quickly as harsh realities press. The young man's "fine wood body was ill strung, and sick even as he sat there to look at" (ibid.). We learn that this particular household has been victimized by the system of "Rehabilitation" that holds out the promise of aid and uplift. The gaze the porch sitters direct out upon the world is full of hatred and anger. The very fact of the unwavering hostility in their eyes (cf. the hostile gazes of the women in the previous episode and of Mrs. Ricketts as cited below), which transfixes Agee "as between spearheads," disrupts the "normal" visual relationships of classic ethnography, where the ethnographer controls the dominant gaze and the natives have no visual agency.

Along with guidance from a cultural insider, the disruption of first impressions is the ethnographic threshold trope most relevant to this episode. And it is Agee's direct encounter with the third occupant of the porch that demonstrates most forcefully how the arriving documentarist is not in control of the situation. This third member of the household, an older man, comes off the porch, apparently unobserved, and suddenly engages Agee physically, surprising him from behind with a shove, indecipherable honking sounds, and a glare from "enraged and terrified eyes" (*FM*, 32). A "thick roil of saliva" hangs in his beard; he is fed and eats like an animal; and Agee connects him metaphorically to brutishness and animalistic sexuality. Later, as they drive away, Agee looks back to see him down on his hands and knees, "coughing like a gorilla" (*FM*, 34).

But this characterization of the older man's mental disability as animal-like is tempered by a second encounter, in which he offers Agee a gift and then watches "affectionately" as this stranger continues his conversation with the other family members. It is at this moment that a small opening for cultural access occurs. In explaining to a confused Agee that the handicapped man wants him to have the proffered magazine, the young woman conveys her awareness of the visitor's limited understanding of their world. But in doing so she makes a personal connection that seems something like a gesture of friendship, "so that happiness burst open inside [Agee] like a flooding of sweet water" (*FM*, 33). What we see here is something closely akin to the moment in reflexive ethnography where the fieldworker recognizes his or her own limited capacity to fathom the cultural realities of the "natives." Anecdotes of confusion, misperception, and faux pas are commonplace in this mode of ethnographic writing, and they often presage breakthroughs in the process of "getting inside."

The third of the quasi-ethnographic vignettes, "Near a Church," both literalizes the attempt-to-gain-access theme and links it to a moment of cultural transgression. Having unintentionally frightened the strolling "negro couple" by thoughtlessly running up behind them, Agee expresses a double remorse. He berates himself for stealing the couple's dignity and squirms in the awareness that he can never adequately convey the depth of his regret and make it right. He has activated defenses in them that irrevocably deny him access to their understanding, much less their friendship. One quality of Agee's documentary axiology that sets it apart from even the most highly developed reflexive ethnographies is his acknowledgment of possible or even inevitable failure. Although difficulties and missteps are reported and dramatized in ethnographies from the 1960s and thereafter, it is a tacit assumption that there will be some measure of ultimate success in gaining access to the interior of the Other. This vignette in *Famous Men* dramatizes absolute failure to get in, constructed as the fieldworker's utter inability to make himself understood. That this event attaches to a direct, material correlative is especially meaningful for the argument that follows here.

The occasion of Agee's "failure" with the strolling couple is the abrupt, roadside stop he and Evans make as they come upon the "paralyzing classicism" of a sun-drenched country church. They have set up the camera and are contemplating a forced entry to the building when the young couple walks by, shaming by their very presence the documentarists' "wish to break into and possess their church" (*FM*, 36). Ironically, Agee's effort to gain permission to enter the building thwarts any chance he might have had of gaining access to the trust of these passersby. The general importance in *Famous Men* of architectural forms, especially vernacular architecture such as this church, and most especially vernacular houses, is so obvious as to need no comment. But the details of how Agee uses the architecture as both setting and symbol deserve more attention. For example, the barred access to the church (and all it stands for) might send us back to architectural thresholds in the other two vignettes. The doorways of their homes is where the sharecroppers first appear in "Late Sunday Morning," and perhaps it is not too great a stretch to assume this is the location from which the women direct their hostile looks at the visitors. And I would propose some significance to the fact that Agee ends "At the Forks" by noting how the woman he has felt some connection with turns away from his departing glance and disappears over the threshold into the house. The larger place of architectural images in *Famous Men* and their relevance to a discussion of ethnographic threshold moments is where I turn next.

I have spent considerable time on the "July 1936" section of *Famous Men* because I find the three vignettes subtly important to the overall moral order of the book.[10] Their relevance is more symbolic than direct, of course. None of them has anything to do with the three tenant families Agee and Evans eventually focus on. Two of them depict meetings with African Americans, despite the explicit assignment to investigate the world of white sharecroppers. All of them dramatize only fleeting encounters, essentially brief roadside stopovers, punctuating automobile trips. What I suggest they have in common is a preoccupation with the complex ethics of cultural entry, and in this they resonate with ethnographic literature contemporary to *Famous Men* and, by virtue of Agee's genius, even more so with work of more recent date. With these brief vignettes as a condensed and highly symbolic introduction to his axiology of entry, Agee anchors his fuller exploration in the houses of the three tenant families, and especially in the Gudgers' dwelling.

Perhaps it is worth noting that the Gudger house appears to be of a distinct type familiar to students of folk architecture. Based on what we can tell from Agee's descriptions and Evans's photographs of the front and rear façades, it seems to be a "double-pen" structure with open central passageway, all covered by a continuous transverse roof. Two internal partitions create four rooms. The back of the structure has been complicated by an L extension and a lean-to addition, though the relation of these to the internal arrangement of rooms is somewhat ambiguous (see plate 16). The front façade is elaborated with a roofed porch and pierced by two symmetrically placed windows. Among the several varieties of traditional, southern, double-pen structures, the Gudger dwelling appears to fall in the category of the so-called dogtrot house.

Evans's photograph of this house front (plate 5) is a beautiful example of the aesthetic strategy that informs many of his *Famous Men* images: the use of seemingly simple symmetries and frank surfaces as a screen for ever more layers of elaboration and complexity. As in most true classicisms, the longer one looks at surface order and simplicity the more complications one sees. Apropos my subject here, there are several things particularly to notice in this photograph. Evans has certainly imposed his own "arbitrated" photographic order on this already highly ordered "façade of summer." Most obviously, he has waited for exactly the moment where the shadows "line up" with the architectural elements, as if they were part of the carpentered plan. The shadow under the eaves fits neatly along the tops of the shuttered windows, and its bottom edge makes a continuous line with the front edge of the porch roof. The shadows at the top of the four porch supports are exactly the same length. Most importantly for my purposes, Evans has waited for the moment where the central rectangle of shadow lines up exactly with the architectural frame of the porch. Or

**Figure 2.1** Walker Evans, "Dog Run of Floyd Burroughs's Home, Hale County, Alabama" 1936

*Source*: Courtesy of Library of Congress, Prints and Photographs Division, FSA-OWI Collection [Reproduction number: LC-USF33-031294-M3].

it lines up *almost* exactly, I should say. When we look closely we see that a thin sliver of light sneaks inside the right-hand porch post and an only slightly larger wedge of shadow escapes on the left. These seemingly trivial departures from otherwise absolute rectilinear order are, in fact, important to my reading of this image as a visual analogue to the ethical concerns in the threshold moments of Agee's text.

On the one hand, Evans's careful photographic arrangement only underscores the clean formal coherence of the architectural façade (Agee characterizes it as "Doric"). It seems to say that one can understand this building, and by implication the lives it encloses, at a single glance. But if we resist the urge to turn the page, where two of its inhabitants await us, we may begin to have doubts about the conceptual "stability" of the house. How exactly does that porch work? One's first inclination, I think, is to see it as receding from us, that is, as an indentation carved out of the front two rooms. This appearance is enhanced by the open passageway, which allows us a view right through the house and out the back. But if we inspect those small "aberrations" of light and shadow mentioned earlier, we see that there is no right angle turn in the front wall of the house. The porch is appended to the front of a continuous surface and projects forward rather than backward.

My point, of course, is that this image constructs a point of entry, indeed the most fundamental of all thresholds, as an ambiguous location. We are at least temporarily confused about where the front boundary of the house is and about the point at which one can be said to have entered. This quality is built into the vernacular form of this particular structure. The central passageway is ambiguously inside *and* outside. No front or back door closes it off to the elements, so it is not really an internal hallway. As Agee tells us, in warm weather it serves almost as another room. However, the failure of an attempt to avoid the unbearable heat of the kitchen by using the passageway as a dining room suggests that this space is somewhat ambiguous even for the Gudgers themselves.[11]

Uncertainty about what is exterior and what is interior, and about how to get from one room to the other, is materialized in the reality of the architecture itself and then underlined in Evans's photograph. I would argue that it is no accident, if perhaps not consciously intended, that the porch he constructs so ambiguously in this image is the very space he and Agee occupy in the three "On the Porch:" episodes, which occur roughly at the beginning, middle, and end of the text. One might suggest that cutting up one nights' continuous experience into these widely separated passages does much the same thing with porch *time*, rendering it ambiguous, as Evans does with porch *space*.

One sees a reduplication of this boundary confusion in a small rhetorical feature of Agee's description of the Gudger house. Some details in his account of the basic arrangement of the structure seem the wrong way round (lean-to kitchen addition on the right; attached wagon shelter on the left) (*FM*, 122). But this is only so if one occupies the point of view from which Evans shoots his photograph, the "natural" observer's position, looking from outside with a front-on orientation. For Agee's description to "work," we must imagine the location of textual production as somehow *from* the house, though it would not be quite right to think of it as *in* the house looking out. It is more nebulous and less geographically specifiable than that. It suggests a kind of conflation between the observer's body and the physical substance of the structure itself, an impression reinforced by the many somatic metaphors Agee uses in describing the building. He later carries this to an extreme when he imagines, paradoxically, experiencing the material reality of the house from the dematerialized perspective of a "disembodied consciousness" (*FM*, 161).

This subtly implied collapse of the subject/object divide is, however, suddenly disrupted when we are abruptly transported to the familiar, outside observer's location to get a look at the façade "square toward the front" (*FM*, 123). Such slippages of descriptive location are textual analogues to the spatial instabilities of Evans's photographs. The long, excruciatingly detailed account of the Gudger house, shocking for its unauthorized invasions of the family's privacy (shocking not least of all to Agee himself) is narratively framed by the departure and return of Annie Mae and her children. They come home to find the deceitful spy Agee "on the front porch with a pencil and an open notebook" (*FM*, 65). The physical location, the acts of (ethnographic) observation and writing, and the moral implications of documentary work parallel and echo one another as boundary phenomena, each one murky, unstable, and ethically conflicted.

All the strands of this discussion so far, the ethnographic tropes discernable in *Famous Men*, the theme of complicated entry, the symbolic significance of the tenant house as the material correlative of ethical uncertainties, come together in the book's climactic section, "Inductions." It is of course consistent with my argument that Agee should make the high point of his documentary text an extended account of first contact, arrival, and entry, specifically, entry to the Gudger house. One qualification I would propose to William Stott's crucial insight that the basic organizing principle of *Famous Men* is "Agee's straining to communicate reality, and failing, and straining again" (Stott, *Documentary Expression*, 310) is that this ultimately unresolved documentary compulsion has as its dominant expression Agee's effort to gain unambiguous access to a coherent and ethically stable interior. Or in more theoretical parlance, his documentary project is to replace his own exteriority with the desired interiority of the Other. "Getting in" physically is the material signifier of bringing the other inside the self. The threshold, literal and metaphorical, is where this problematic transference is most at issue and where the documentary transaction is most ethically fraught.[12]

Agee employs purposeful redundancy to emphasize that the final and climactic "act" of the book (it follows the "Intermission: Conversation in the Lobby" section) is the primary point of entry and true beginning to his documentary/ethnographic experience. The section heading "Inductions," that is, "leadings in" or initiations, is followed immediately by a simple statement of what the whole text has been moving toward: "I remember so well, the first night I spent under one of these roofs" (*FM*, 319). The key importance of the inaugural moment is further urged by the redundant and oddly positioned subheadings, "*First*" and, down two lines and across the page, "*First meeting*." Later in the section Agee rings yet another change on the theme of beginnings when he applies the liturgical term *"Introit"* and then *"Second Introit"* as headings for the two most important scenes in the whole pattern of threshold moments: his first arrival at the Gudger house, where he shelters from a violent thunderstorm, and then his return later that night after his car bogs down in the unpaved track linking the tenant farmsteads to the outside world. I will return to these crucial scenes in a moment.

First, though, we need to back up to the beginning of the "Inductions" section, where we have a scene of literal first contact. In one of its ideal scenarios, ethnographic work follows a trajectory from some chance encounter, through mounting layers of tentative reconnaissance and negotiation, to a "crisis point" of entry, and proceeding from there to increasing degrees of acceptance and even "disappearance" into some taken-for-granted, unmarked identity as a full citizen of the community, the holy grail of academic, participant-observation fieldwork. Carried to its extreme, this movement can lead to another kind of crisis point; that at which one "goes native" and abandons the observer/ethnographer identity altogether. Agee never comes near such a conclusion, of course, but whether he makes it past the point of entry at all is a complicated question in itself.

In following something similar to the afore mentioned scenario, Agee also echoes, no doubt unwittingly, some conventions of characterization from what I have been loosely invoking as the ethnographic tradition. To say that the "cast of characters" in *Famous Men* includes figures, who display traces of genre origins, is perhaps only to restate the point Agee himself makes by introducing his real life "subjects" at the beginning of the book as if on a playbill roster. This in no way contradicts one of Stott's other main points about the significance of *Famous Men* in thirties documentary, namely, that Agee explodes the prevailing conventions by depicting actual people rather than stock types or poverty icons (*Documentary Expression*, 291–92). They have profound inner lives and clear, if unreflexive, aesthetic sensibilities. Agee was painfully and obsessively aware that in writing about these people and their world he was inevitably "falsifying" them. One of the fundamental tenets of so-called textualist ethnography in the 1980s, and after, is the acknowledgment that even the most clinical of documentary accounts is a filtering screen rather than a transparent window.[13] That screen is woven from the traces of myriad conventions, tropes, narrative expectations, genre patterns, indeed, from the whole discursive environment of the prevailing culture. The gist of my argument is that the patterns of Agee's screen have much in common with the textual practices of ethnography, past and present. This includes his representations of the people he so desperately and futilely wished to portray in their absolute, human particularity.

"Inductions" opens with Agee exiting a small-town courthouse to find Evans in conversation with the voluble Fred Ricketts. Bud Woods and George Gudger soon join them. As we follow the development of the relationships among these five men, we may discern at least the ghosts of recurring ethnographic figures. Ricketts, "crazy, clownish, foxy" (*FM*, 68), is the perhaps too talkative and too quickly friendly indigene whose gregariousness in this situation comes partly from his inclination to assume these strangers are "Government men." He continues to play the role of slightly comical, and even foolish, facilitator of Agee's and Evans's endeavors. But his nervous, unguarded friendliness overlays, in Agee's understanding of him, a painful longing not to be harmed or ridiculed more than he already has been by the world these visitors represent. Agee affords Ricketts the dignity of this complexity while placing him in the role of native mediator who enables contact but who represents a superficial level of encounter.

Importantly, this moment of first contact is marked by another inaugural gesture found in ethnographic discourse. Evans takes some surreptitious photographs of the unsuspectingly naïve Ricketts, who is distracted by conversation with Agee. This might be read as another kind of threshold moment, the point at which ethnographic original sin occurs. Agee invokes the familiar trope of the camera as a hostile apparatus, "a weapon, a stealer of images and souls, a gun, an evil eye" (*FM*, 320). We may think back to the "Late Sunday Morning" episode, where the camera and documentary victimization are fleetingly linked. Ricketts is victimized here only mildly and without much obvious harm. Nevertheless, it is an importantly emblematic moment in *Famous Men*'s documentary axiology, in that it anticipates in miniature the agonizing self-interrogation and ethical critique Agee conducts so relentlessly throughout. Of course we have already witnessed most of this axiological drama by the time we reach its opening act here.

Agee is quite explicit that the camera is a key symbolic artifact of *Famous Men*. On the one hand, he aspires to achieve in his writing the seeming directness this device invites us to assume about its operations and results. However, it is also an apparatus of automatic subterfuge. I have said earlier that the camera is the second, along with the tenant house, of the key threshold artifacts. Agee himself links the two at a telling moment. Just after the Gudger family has left, and he is setting about to violate the threshold of their privacy by moving through the undefended house "as they would trust [him] not to move," we get this image:

> The silence of the brightness of this middle morning is increased upon me moment by moment and upon this house, and upon this house the whole of heaven is drawn into one lens; and this house itself in each of its objects, it, too, is one lens. I am being made witness to matters no human being may see. (*FM*, 120)

The house, then, becomes the scene of a crime recorded, or perhaps even perpetrated, through what I take to be the metaphorical lens of a camera, which documents things that should not and could not otherwise be seen. The camera, of course, literally does allow the visual capture of what the naked eye cannot grasp. In this, it stands for the illicit transgression of the threshold, the criminal appropriation of an interiority

Agee has no right to. He is fully aware that his actions constitute a kind of moral burglary (see below), close kin to that other invasive activity, mentioned earlier: spying.

Like the door of the house, the lens of the camera is an ambiguous threshold. Its ethical standing is inherently unstable. The play between interior and exterior is just as slippery here as it is in Agee's relation to the Gudger dwelling. Doing full justice to the documentary task, as he so uncompromisingly sees it, means gaining complete access to the interiors of other beings, but this is both ultimately impossible and ethically tainted. The paradox is that such entry always entails a degree of transgression, and Agee's tortured awareness of his violation leaves him always with one foot outside, trapped in his own exteriority. The camera may be understood as a counterpart or complement to this paradox, its symbolic "reverse shot," so to speak. Its lens is the threshold across which an exterior reality is seemingly pulled into interior space. The paradigm of the camera obscura, the darkened room into which the outside world is vividly projected, has been much discussed.[14] Suffice it here to say that the camera as inherently a thief of Otherness, hoarding its plunder in an interior archive of images, is another form of threshold transgression.

We see this ethical ambiguity of the ethnographer's camera being further enacted in the scene immediately following the meeting outside the courthouse. Agee and Evans offer to drive the three men home, and this becomes the occasion for a picture-taking session on the Ricketts side porch. We have here an elaborated variation on the ethnographic arrival scene already invoked in the "Late Sunday Morning" episode (cf. Spiegel, *James Agee and the Legend*, 99). In this case, the furtive gathering of the native children, both shy and playful in their innocence, is the familiar convention. Fred Ricketts's foolish eagerness to stage-manage the picture taking, shouting for his children and sending for the Woods and Gudger families, displays his obliviousness to what is really going on. His wife, however, is onto the visitors immediately, and Agee's recognition of her awareness makes him especially intent on communicating with her. He acknowledges the "strangeness of meaning and precariousness of balance" in this threshold moment, which he wishes "so much as never before to make secure," above all for the silently resistant Sadie Ricketts. In other words, the conflicted ethics of this arrival moment are coded in the deployment of the camera, and Mrs. Ricketts is the figure who registers this for Agee. Retrospectively, he addresses her directly:

> and to you it was as if you and your children and your husband and these others were stood there naked in front of the cold absorption of the camera in all your shame and pitiableness to be pried into and laughed at; and your eyes were wild with fury and shame and fear. (*FM*, 321)

Though he yearns to allay her suspicions and communicate his good will, there is an irreducible kernel of truth to the perception Agee imagines for her.

These first contact and arrival scenes are immediately followed by the also familiar "negotiation" phase of the classic ethnographic process (cf. Spiegel, *James Agee and the Legend*, 101–102). Here too, the shadow of an ethnographic character type may be dimly discerned, in this case hovering behind the flesh and blood figure of Bud Woods. Agee and Evans follow their first visit to the Ricketts's place with subsequent trips over the next weeks. They discover that the fifty-nine-year-old Woods, the eldest in this small community of farm families, father-in-law to Gudger and brother-in-law to Ricketts, is the real key to the success of their work. They discover him to be the "shrewdest and wisest" and the one to whom they can eventually reveal themselves "fully." This is possible at least partly because he most shares their "reflective and skeptical cast of mind" and, in some measure, their politics (*FM*, 327–28).

In short, Woods occupies the ethnographic role of the wise elder who, after careful consideration, puts his requisite stamp of approval on the ethnographic project and sets its terms.[15]

It is Woods who decides that Agee and Evans will move in with the Gudgers; and, presumably, he weighs in on the financial arrangements, the significance of which is often, as in this case, downplayed in ethnographic texts. The most relevant trope invoked here is another threshold moment, that place where the authoritative insider assigns the ethnographer an identity understandable in indigenous terms. Agee enacts a classic form of this convention when he tells Woods, in syntactically tortured retrospect: " you became in what our whole lives were then involved in a sort of father to us, with this half-recognized yet never made open among the three of us" (*FM*, 327). The three tenant families form a kinship network, one of anthropology's stocks in trade, and the two outsiders are symbolically allowed into it. However, their tacit acceptance as kin heightens rather than resolves Agee's continuing struggle with other, more problematic thresholds.

We finally come to what in my view is the true center of *Famous Men*: two scenes of literal first entry to the Gudger house, the first and second "introits." Agee confirms their importance in several ways. One is his narrative manipulation, placing his account of these events not near the book's beginning, its proper place in the "real time" chronology, but almost at the end. In doing so, Agee reproduces the "correct" *ethnographic* sequence, according to which the first entry to the house, first meal there, and first night's sleep under its roof symbolically mark the culmination of the process of "getting in" that began with the first contact scenes.

Also, Agee elaborately prepares for this climactic threshold day with a long interlude where he seeks relief from his fieldwork by taking a trip to the city, a "return to the metropole" motif that one might also relate to the tradition of narrative ethnography. This sojourn sets up an inchoate longing that drives Agee back to his field site and then coalesces as a specific wish to visit the tenant families, and particularly to see George Gudger. He has begun to recognize in this man the possibility of special fellowship. "He was the most direct talker and seemed the sorest and most intelligent" (*FM*, 340). In Gudger we may catch echoes of yet a third character type from ethnographic writing, the indigenous double, the cultural insider who is most like the ethnographer and becomes the special friend, confidant, and key source of information. Of the three men, Gudger is the only one roughly of Agee's generation. We learn in earlier sections about things they have in common, for example, their shared but suppressed and unspoken sexual attraction to Gudger's young sister-in-law. Although there are also ways that the Gudgers occupy parental roles for Agee and Evans, Woods is the real paterfamilias, making George the protective "older brother."[16]

The most obvious way that Agee underscores the importance of the two scenes of entry to the Gudger home is by explicitly announcing them as a complementary pair of "dreams come true" (*FM*, 344). One is the wild, apocalyptic scene where Agee and Ricketts find refuge in the Gudger bedroom during a violent thunderstorm; the other the tranquil late-night meal provided for Agee when he walks back to the Gudger house after his car becomes hopelessly mired. Both these episodes might be viewed in relation to the last of the ethnographic tropes I will mention: the scene of shipwreck and marooning. Obviously derived from numerous literary sources, including travel and exploration narratives and popular novels, its most classic form in ethnography is the moment when the fieldworker finds him or herself left alone in an alien culture, bereft of guide or mediating helper and without means of escape.[17] It is the moment at which the ethnographer is most vulnerable, most emotionally distressed, and most in need of aid. Not infrequently, it leads to some sort of breakthrough in the process of gaining access. That is certainly so in this case.

Agee and Ricketts arrive at the Gudgers with the downpour at their heels. They shelter on the porch, where Agee says he was inclined to stay, perhaps foreshadowing his later occupation of this symbolic location. Gudger comes out, though, and ushers them down the passageway to the locked door of the main bedroom. They are let in to find the whole family fearfully and silently waiting out the deluge. This becomes the occasion for perhaps Agee's farthest entry into the lives of these people, even though at this point they are still quite new to him, and he has yet to develop the everyday familiarity and easy affection that only extended contact can bring. The several pages in which he describes the scene and monitors the subtly shifting emotional atmosphere are some of the finest in the book. It is an account of what an anthropologist might call *communitas*, one of those special cultural occasions where individual identities, social roles, and hierarchies of power fade and the awareness of undifferentiated common humanity takes over.[18] In such moments the boundary of the self opens to all others.

Agee is for this brief moment more truly "in the room" than at any other time, but the experience is fleeting. Even as he registers the subtlest qualities of collective feeling, the ethical taint seeps in. This registers particularly in his exchange of glances with the Gudger daughter, Louise. Although their communication has been entirely through their eyes, Agee suddenly senses he may have inappropriately crossed some boundary with this young girl, bringing an unintentional threat. He finds he cannot read in her face a response to his "violation," and in the end it is he who breaks off the tacit communication and looks away (*FM*, 353–54).

The single loveliest moment in this section comes as the storm ends and the spell is broken:

the personality of a room, and of a group of creatures, has undergone a change, as if of two different techniques or mediums; what began as "rembrandt," [*sic*] deeplighted in gold, in each interger colossally heavily planted, has become a photograph, a record in clean, staring, colorless light, almost without shadow, . . . a family of tenant farmers, late in a sunday [*sic*] afternoon, in a certain fold of country, in a certain part of the south, and of the lives of each of them, confronted by a person strange to them, whose presence and its motives are so outlandish there is no reason why any of it should be ever understood; almost as if there were no use trying to explain; just say, I am from Mars, and let it go at that. (*FM*, 357)

The relevance of this scene's resolution into a black and white photograph and of Agee's self-identification with extreme exteriority, literally in the form of otherworldliness, perhaps needs no further elaboration. Nor will I dwell long, in conclusion, over the other of the climactic entry scenes. When Agee returns to the Gudgers' house late that night, he has literally been stranded. The offer of a meal is perhaps the most basic symbol of cultural entry in ethnographic discourse. I would only note that Agee takes this inaugural meal, however sacramental, in one of those ambiguous spaces of the vernacular house, the open passageway that is neither exactly outside nor inside. And when given a bed it is, of course, not in the collective family bedroom, but in the front "parlor" bedroom, where Agee is left alone with the alienating discomforts of a thin mattress and attacking bedbugs, fleas, and lice. He goes out, naked, to the front porch to urinate, and then into the front yard, where he turns to look at the house and feels "like a special sort of burglar" (*FM*, 375, cf. Spiegel, *James Agee and the Legend*, 115–16).

As a final word about the symbolic significance of the spaces in the Gudger house, I will only point out that the room Agee occupies in the two sections that conclude "Inductions" ("In the room: the Testament" and "In the room: In bed") is itself ambiguous. It is not a part of everyday life for the family. As often in vernacular dwellings, it is a space reserved for special uses, such as entertaining higher status visitors or as guest sleeping quarters. Often special objects are kept there, such as the family bible Agee finds that first night. Like the room across the passageway, which is used for storage and has its exterior door permanently nailed shut, this parlor/bedroom has no ceiling, or window glass or screens, leaving it susceptible to the invasion of the elements and vermin. We have learned earlier that the children sometimes sleep here, but mostly the family inhabits the back two rooms. Though Agee sleeps in a room under the roof of this house, it is not a really all the way "inside." That he soon shifts his sleeping quarters to the porch is just a clearer expression of his marginality.

It is noteworthy that when Agee arrives late at night back at the Gudgers, the dog snarls at him from this porch and George confronts him angrily. It turns out, Agee tells us, "He had thought I was a nigger" (*FM*, 363). We have also seen how Agee and Evans were earlier mistaken for "Government men." These are not, I think, unrelated misperceptions, unrelated, that is, either to each other or to the general axiology of entry. The agent of state power and the most powerless of the poor by virtue of race are the outer limits of otherness available to the direct experience of *Famous Men's* white tenant farmers.

The role of the ethnographer/documentarist partakes of both power and powerlessness. The former ensures some level of access to the lives of others. The two visitors are on a subsidized assignment; they can travel at will; they can pay for a place from which to observe and document, not to mention spy and eavesdrop. They are also, however, powerless to get all the way across the threshold, and they are inevitably trapped in irresolvable ethical dilemmas. *Famous Men* ends with the final installment of Agee's nighttime reverie as he lies on that multiple ambiguous front porch. From there he listens to sounds of the family within and to a mysterious call without, a double perception that could hardly be more apt.

The complexity and ambivalence with which Agee addresses these issues cannot be overstated. For example, his self-indictment over spying in the Gudger home must be viewed in relation to his other invocation of this identity, as expressed in his poem "To Walker Evans" at the beginning of the book. There he styles himself and Evans as spies in the mode of Edgar in *King Lear*, feigning madness to "move delicately among the enemy" until the time when they can reveal themselves as servants of righteousness and scourges of the dominant evil. In other words, they are double agents, conducting documentary surveillance on the defenseless poor, but with the deeper purpose of subverting the forces that both create the poverty and subsidize their documentation of it.

Likewise, the home invasion through which Agee "steals" the remarkable inventory of spaces, surfaces, objects, smells in the "Shelter" section is the most blatant and egregious transgression of thresholds. But this act of uninvited entry serves the higher purpose of getting us at least a little way into the aesthetic radiance of the lives this dwelling shelters and expresses. An important counterpart to this physical violation of literal boundaries is Agee's lyrically imagined, X-ray penetration of the wall separating him from the sleeping Gudger family in the "A Country Letter" section:

> and thus I know they rest and the profundity of their tired-ness, as if I were in each one of these seven bodies whose sleeping I can almost touch through this wall, and which in the darkness I so clearly see with the whole touch and weight of my body (*FM*, 51)

The conflation of seeing and physically touching, indeed, corporeally merging with the bodies of the family ("I lie down inside each one" [*FM*, 52]), expresses the transcendent goal of all Agee's efforts, a goal ultimately unachievable under the conditions of material existence we all inhabit.

## NOTES

1. In the Agee/Evans text the photographs are not numbered or captioned. I follow the convention of considering each photographic page a plate, applying continuous numbering. All my references to the text, both images and prose, use James Agee and Walker Evans, *Let Us Now Praise Famous Men* ([1941] Boston and New York: Houghton Mifflin, 2001). All subsequent references are to this edition and are located within the text.

2. T. V. Reed (1988) has made an effective case for considering *Famous Men* a postmodern work "*avant la lettre*," or more specifically, a work of "postmodern realism." He argues that "its heterogeneity and pastichelike qualities are postmodernist," and, especially relevant to the present discussion, that "it engages the epistemological problematic of postmodernism as well" (157).

3. As seen in Jay Ruby, *A Crack in the Mirror: Reflexive Perspectives in Anthropology* (Philadelphia: University of Pennsylvania Press. 1982).

4. James. S. Miller, "Inventing the 'Found' Object: Artifactuality, Folk History, and the Rise of Capitalist Ethnography in 1930s America," *Journal of American Folklore* 117 (2004): 373–393.

5. I am not suggesting anywhere in this chapter that Agee consciously drew on the work of university-based cultural anthropology. To my knowledge he did not concern himself with the professional ethnographic practices of social scientists. Modern cultural anthropology in particular, with participant-observation fieldwork as its defining methodology, had only really emerged in the 1920s. The tropes and conventions I am concerned with are part of the general cultural inheritance of direct-observation nonfiction in the 1930s and thereafter. To trace their sources and cognates in other periods and genres is far too large a task to undertake here. It is what Agee does with these shared literary resources that concerns me. The more "official" ethnographic tradition provides, I believe, a useful comparative window through which to view *Famous Men.*

6. On what he calls the "axiographics" of documentary film, see Bill Nichols, *Representing Reality* (Bloomington: Indiana University Press, 1991), 76–103.

7. Mary Louise Pratt, "Fieldwork in Common Places," in *Writing Culture*, ed. Clifford and Marcus, 27–50.(Berkeley: University of California Press, 1886).

8. One roughly contemporary text that could repay comparison to *Famous Men* is Zora Neale Hurston's *Mules and Men* (1935). Although quite a different kind of ethnography/documentary, written in a different register, and treated with a much lighter hand, its collection of folktales from "the Negro farthest down" overlays a subtle subtext of ethnographic reflexivity. In its arrival scenes it too opens up a literary space for ethical considerations.

9. For examples see David Maybury-Lewis, *The Savage and the Innocent* (Cleveland: World Publishing, 1965 and 1967); Paul Rabinow, *Symbolic Domination: Cultural Form and Historical Change in Morocco* (Chicago: University of Chicago Press, 1975 and 1977); and Jean-Paul Dumont, *Under the Rainbow* (Austin: University of Texas Press, 1976 and 1978).

10. This is perhaps the appropriate place to mention that it was only after completing a draft of this chapter that I read Alan Spiegel's compelling chapter on *Famous Men* in his critical study, *James Agee and the Legend of Himself* (Columbia: University of Missouri Press, 1998).

  Although we start from quite different places and arrive at different places, if not entirely incompatible conclusions, I find a number of central points coincide. For example, he too offers an extended commentary on the "July 1936" episodes (Spiegel, 91–95), highlighting a number of the elements I mention here. Also, we both link these early episodes to the climactic "Inductions" section. Our arguments share the opinion that this section, perhaps the most important (and moving) in the book, is key to understanding the deep coherence of Agee's text. With this as a general acknowledgment that Spiegel precedes me in some of my independently arrived at views, I will make further note of places where our discussions cross paths especially clearly.

11. For a discussion of double-pen vernacular house types and a definitive examination of the use of spaces in such dwellings, see Michael Ann Williams, *Homeplace: The Social Use and Meaning of Folk Dwelling in Southwestern North Carolina* (Charlottesville: University of Virginia Press, 1991).

12. Spiegel reads *Famous Men* as a modernist quest narrative, a quest born of desire to return to origins, to security, to the source of creative energies, in short, a desire to return "home." The Gudger household is the principal object of this desire, which is both a nostalgic yearning and a psychosexual regression to childhood that, in Spiegel's interpretation, gives Agee the aesthetic grounding to produce his masterpiece. This reading is not incompatible with the one I offer here. In some sense the classic ethnographic process entails the desire to gain access to a place that is somehow "prior" to the ethnographer's own moment, to a world more basic or primitive or "pure." My interpretation, I hasten to add, diverges from Spiegel's over whether Agee really succeeds in reaching the object of his desire. See below for a discussion of the familiar motif in participant-observation ethnography whereby the fieldworker is assigned the role of child or dependent in the indigenous kinship system.

13. James Clifford and George E. Marcus, eds. *Writing Culture: The Poetics and Politics of Ethnography* (Berkeley: University of California Press, 1986).

14. Jonathan Crary, *Techniques of the Observer: On Vision and Modernity in the Nineteenth Century* (Cambridge, MA: MIT Press. 1993), 25–66.

15. Marcel Griaule, *Conversations with Ogotemmêli: An Introduction to Dogon Religious Ideas* (London: Oxford University Press, 1965).

16. Looking back again to the poem at the beginning of *Famous Men*, Agee refers to himself and Evans as "younger sons." Given his interpretation of Agee's experience as a kind of childhood regression, Spiegel emphasizes the parental qualities of the Gudgers. I find this to be somewhat overstated, but in any case, as symbolic constructions the social roles and relationships in question are not absolutely fixed.

17. The most famous expression of this motif in the anthropological literature is no doubt Bronislaw Malinowski's 1922 commentary on the nature of participant-observation fieldwork: "Imagine yourself suddenly set down surrounded by all your gear, alone on a tropical beach close to a native village, while the launch or dinghy which has brought you sails away out of sight." Bronisla Malinowski, *Argonauts of the Western Pacific* ([1922] New York: E. P. Dutton, 1961).

    He goes on to describe a general process of ethnographic "getting in" against which one could instructively map Agee's experience.

18. Victor Turner, *Dramas, Fields, and Metaphors: Symbolic Action in Human Society* (Ithaca, NY: Cornell University Press, 1974).

3

# WALKER EVANS'S CONTRAPUNTAL DESIGN: THE SEQUENCES OF PHOTOGRAPHS IN THE FIRST AND SECOND EDITIONS OF *LET US NOW PRAISE FAMOUS MEN*

*Alan Trachtenberg*

Walker Evans's photographs might better be called fictions than documents, or even *documentary* fictions. Their mode is self-abnegation, the cherished detachment and withholding of signs of the author's person that Evans learned from Flaubert and James and Joyce and other masters of modern writing. Evans called his method "documentary style." It is the look of objectivity, of directness, simplicity, and vernacular authenticity, that gives his pictures their persuasive authority. But that look, of course, is another kind of pose that disguises more complex purposes beyond merely to record the surface appearance of things. Intentions beyond literal documentary show up in the way Evans published and arranged his 1930s pictures, their order on the page, and the relations among them: structures of organization neither narrative nor thematic but something closer to a dialogic form of interaction, images in conversation with each other.

The best achievement of sequencing is the intricate, subtle, and contrapuntal form in *American Photographs*, where

Evans's formal patterning shapes the book as a constant play
of part and whole, image in dialogue with image to make visible a culture dense with overlapping and intersecting signs
and signals, codes, and presumptions. The pictured world is
made up of things, people, signs, and pictures: the everyday
world in grand and miniscule detail. Traces of the making
of art—pictures, signs, patterns—pervade the pictured things
and activities of the book, the book's subject matter mimick-
ing the book's own activity of photographic representation. It
is a book about art and artifact, about the countless activities
of making and building that represent the tangible America
of the title.

Sequence in *American Photographs* helps us see what is
afoot in the patterning of the photographs in the two editions
of *Let Us Now Praise Famous Men* (1941). In both editions the
flow of pictures has a discrete relation to the rest of the book.
They are set apart as "Book One," a wryly self-mocking device
whereby all the photographs appear in a self-contained port-
folio preceding the title page: "Book One" in the sense that
the pictures belong at once together as a "book" of its own,
and have a place, indeterminate as it may be, within or anent
the larger book authored jointly, though, we learn, unequally,
by "James Agee and Walker Evans." A second edition in 1960,
after Agee's death in 1955, retained the fiction of "Book
One," but allowed Evans more freedom; sacrificing the tight-
ness and intensity of the 1941 sequence, he added thirty-one
additional photographs. In the first edition, the photographs
are arranged by family (each of the "three tenant families"
of Agee's text) into three sections, each separated by a blank
page. The 1960 edition expands the family sections, changes
some of the images while adding new ones and different crops
of some of the earlier images, and adds a fourth section that
widens the horizon of the sequence in significant ways: ter-
ritorially, beyond Hale County, and thematically, beyond the
constellation of the rude cabins that define the domain of
the three impoverished sharecropper families. By its gestures
toward the elsewheres that hover just beyond the edge of the

domain of the families, the fourth section notably enlarges the role of the photographs (and of Evans himself) in the text as a whole.

A key element of the old pre-Depression myth of the South had been the idea that farmers were yeoman, proud tillers of the soil rewarded by nature and a benign government with an adequate living and well-being. They stood, in the myth, for the virtue that comes with closeness to the soil; they assured the health and continuity of the republic. The tenant lien system flew in the face of this Jeffersonian myth, and the photographs and research sponsored by the Farm Security Administration showed that system to be a form of peonage all the more cruel for its mockery of the myth of the yeoman farmer as bulwark of the republic. The sharecropping system held its victims, white and black, in unremitting poverty. Neither Agee nor Evans wished merely to expose the wickedness of the system or to further diminish the humanity of their subjects by reducing them to the status of pathetic victims. While Agee struggled openly to find an appropriate point of view toward the tenant families, Evans's pictures perform a near-miracle of balance: poverty made painfully visible but pride and grace displayed as counterpoint to the hardscrabble daily existence.

Agee and Evans together show that the dispossessed families possess something of their own. There is the world given to them, an existence of deprivation, but repossessed as something of their own; by gestures such as their keeping snapshots on the walls and placing crockery pots where they look best, they make of someone else's property something of their own. Each of the three family sections of photographs in both editions consists of single and group portraits set within expanding spheres of daily life and work: the cabins, their furnishings, the surrounding yards and fields. Each picture gives its own particular exactitude of observation. The first sequence, opening with the standing portrait of the landlord, introduces the system within which the families live, the system of tenancy represented by that figure in a rumpled suit who fills the entire frame—a large man, shrewd in his face and eyes, a figure whose afterimage pervades the sequence. He is the unshakable reminder of the governing *system*: private property, absentee landlordism, and exploitative tenancy.

Each of the family sequences shows individuals alone and grouped together. Not without tensions and complications in their familial relations, they take possession of each other and of their physical spaces; the walls, the floors, the bed, the tables, and the cooking utensils all express daily use and patterns of family life: relations between man and wife, between parents and children, and between individual and family and the wider unseen world eventually brought into the picture in the 1960 edition.

The fourth section added in 1960 opens with an unexpected shift of location and perspective, from the cloisterlike confines of the family cabins and outbuildings to the main street of a country town. The final image of the preceding section serves as transition: a view from the rear of one of the tenants with some of his family in a wagon pulled by a pair of mules, on their way to town (we deduce) with a load of freshly picked cotton. Suddenly we are in what seems another world—a paved street, automobiles and pickup trucks slanted diagonally at the curb, shops, stores, pedestrians with shoes and clean clothes—we realize that Evans is supplementing the story of the three tenant families as depicted in the first edition, an expanded story in which contrast and connection with outside institutions and forces become visible and palpable. The sequence of nineteen new images gives an inventory of the town and beyond—the South within which the story of the three families is now told again with greater social nuance. We see signs of communal life, a mayor's office, schools, fire hydrants, a post office, a railroad station, a city boarding house, a ruined plantation mansion, all bearing on the lives of the three families. And we see their fellow Southerners with dark skin, segregated but part of the same scene, the same streets, and the same shops.

The presence of blacks filtered through a Southern imagination appears especially in a stunning picture that follows directly after the image of a down-at-the-heels plantation house. In the picture showing two mules, a brick wall, and a torn minstrel poster, Evans portrays a quiet event in the shimmering heat of a high-noon sun. The poet Donald Justice, himself a Southerner from Florida, was once stopped cold by this picture and wrote a poem he later placed within a sequence he called "My South." He might well be speaking for Evans too.

The poem, "Mule Team and Poster," opens with flat descriptions: two mules stand in front of a brick wall. They are hitched to a flatbed wagon whose wheels have spokes that resemble (in the poem's few pointed metaphors) wooden flowers pulled from mud. Dried mud says that rains have passed through here recently and that the sun is now back, "with a special brightness, like God." But it is the poster that the poem sharpens its focus upon with another stirring metaphor: the torn poster clinging to the wall looks "as though a huge

**Figure 3.1**  Walker Evans, "Minstrel Poster in Alabama Town, 1936"

*Source*: Courtesy of Library of Congress, Prints and Photographs Division, FSA-OWI Collection [Reproduction number: LC-USF342001134-A].

door stood open / or a terrible flap of brain had been peeled
back." What is revealed is "someone's idea of heaven," dancing
girls in ringed dresses and bobbed hair. "Meanwhile the mules
crunch patiently the few corn shucks / someone has patiently
scattered for them." Who is that someone who scattered the
corn and the someone with the idea of heaven as black dancing
girls kicking up their legs? No matter. The poem concludes
with the sun dropping "a long shadow" beneath the wagon,
"like a great scythe laid down there and forgotten."[1]

Poem and photograph both hinge on the relation between
the commonplace world represented by the mule and the world
of romantic fantasy depicted in the minstrel poster. These are
separate but joined perspectives by which, as the poem leads
us to recognize, the photograph composes its own fiction. The
fantasy performed behind the back of the mule munching its
meal tells the whole story.

Justice's poem helps us to see how Evans sees, the way his
photographic eye works, how it creates the fiction of a place by
giving the viewer things in space, in time, and in the imagination at once and together. People are absent but their presence
is traced by the poem: the someone who scattered corn shucks
for the mules, and the someone who had an idea of heaven
and made a picture, a minstrel poster, out of it. And the
someone who owns the mules and wagons and the labor they
perform, the warehouse in which the products of that labor—
probably bales of cotton—are stored until taken to market and
exchanged for cash. A tense balance of opposites, then: dreams
and realities, minstrel poster and brick wall, unseen laborers
and owners, mules and wagon, pavement and street, all perceived by photograph and poem as a unified whole, a harmony
of parts yoked together by someone's eye for the beauty that is
truth on a hot, still, summer day in Alabama.

The noon sun drops a shadow beneath the wagon, a meager
bit of shade in the shape of a scythe, sign of the grim reaper,
emblem of time and death, of things passing away. The poem
glosses the photograph as if it were a constructed or invented
fiction, the fiction of a "South" where eloquent brick walls

sing erotic dreams of a heaven where racial boundaries are there to be transgressed, while shadows proclaim that nothing lasts forever. Put the three families back into the picture, imagine them as part of the same fiction the South projects of itself, and we can see why we may wonder whether Evans just found this picture of Southern reality in the 1930s or made it up, whether it is his literal document or his work of art. "Lyrical document" describes it best. In his pictures arrayed in sequence, ordinary things glow with the revelation of historical-poetical truth.

## NOTE

1. Donald Justice "Mule Team and Poster," in *The Sunset Maker* (Greenwich: Anvil Press, 1987).

# 4

# THE TYRANNY OF WORDS IN THE ECONOMY OF ABUNDANCE: MODERNISM, LANGUAGE, AND POLITICS IN *LET US NOW PRAISE FAMOUS MEN*

*Sue Currell*

To some observers in the late 1930s, the problems faced by the sharecroppers of the South were as much symptoms of a general linguistic failure and breakdown as they were illustrative of political and social inertia. Indeed, the two were closely connected. In 1929 the modernist Eugene Jolas noted the connection between social collapse and linguistic inertia when he stated, "[t]he Art of expression is suffering from a paralysis that is one of the symptoms of a civilization in collapse."[1] As this chapter shows, James Agee's fraught attempts to dissect, understand, and revive the power of language in *Let Us Now Praise Famous Men* paralleled a popular exploration of linguistic structures and the political role of language in the New Deal era. With the rise of fascism in Europe, language and the control over meaning and language became a matter of heightened interest to writers and politicians and led to an accumulating interest in the relationship between semantics and politics over the period in which Agee penned his book. Even writers who had no interest in the creation of literary masterpieces, or the apparent abstractions of artistic modernism, held in common with Agee the desire to explore the political failure of language and communication. In 1938 the New Deal economic observer Stuart Chase argued for a language revolution, stating in *The Tyranny of Words* that it was linguistic and semantic failure that had lead to "slums, *Tobacco Roads*, and undernourished, ragged schoolchildren in a land of potential economic plenty."[2] Just as the New Deal in government had demanded a "recovery" through experimentation with political structures, the exploration of linguistic structures and functions now promised to alter the way meaning was produced on the page (and by logical extension, to alter certain social and political realities).

For avant-garde writers and literary scholars understanding semantic structures had always carried political importance for the nation. Ezra Pound argued in 1934 that "If a nation's literature declines, the nation atrophies and decays," thus efforts were needed "to understand the function of language, and to understand why a tolerance for slipshod expression in whatever department of writing gradually leads to chaos, munitions-profiteers, [and] the maintenance of wholly unnecessary misery."[3] Not only does an examination of the intersection between language and politics in the 1930s shed greater light on the political aesthetics of *Famous Men*, it illustrates the important currency of avant-garde experiments concerning language to social and political discourse of the time. To Agee, words had a "power of deceit" that was "vertiginous," something in which all artists, journalists, and propagandists colluded to enact social and psychological control over others.[4] Breaking free of those aesthetic conventions that misled and deceived—whether they came from capitalism (*Fortune* magazine) or the New Deal, or even Marxism—truly equated, to Agee, to freedom from oppression. Freeing words, then, was freeing Americans from the inability to change reality. Yet, as Agee comes to realize through writing *Famous Men*, it is the limits of freedom through communication, and therefore the limits of language as democracy, that his experiment finally reveals.

It is in the variety of ways that *Famous Men* has been interpreted that we can most clearly see the tensions within Agee's textual politics. To simplify the critical trends: *Famous Men* is seen on the one hand as a "withdrawal from political discourse" or as modernist solipsism, variously interpreted as a retreat from politics into abstraction, providing a map of language definitely not usable by either the political left of the period or the capitalist employers at *Fortune* magazine.[5] Similarly, the book is considered as a withdrawal into the Freudian subconscious, even onanistic, an autobiographical monument to the author's encounter with the primal scene, "which did not in fact have anything to do with the tenants themselves."[6] In this view, *Famous Men* presents an antidocumentary and is consequently apolitical. It cannot function as political rhetoric because it is either too personal or too abstract and experimental. On the other hand, *Famous Men* is lauded as *the* representative text of the 1930s, the height of exploration into documentary aesthetics and political expose of poverty of the era.[7] Further to this it is perceived as a cutting iconoclastic expose of the patronizing attempts by mass culture to depict social problems. In this same vein, others have seen the book as a "failed" attempt at politics, one that illustrates the political compromises of the author who famously worked for *Fortune* (and therefore capitalism) and yet who sees himself as "a Communist by sympathy and conviction" (*FM*, 249). Indeed, English professor James Miller contends that *FM* "came to underwrite a particular and highly overdetermined narrative of corporate-capitalist 'progress": In his attempt to reify the folk object over the mass produced, he argues, Agee merely ends up renewing the capitalist object for reconsumption within the mass market.[8]

In *New Deal Modernism*, Michael Szalay likewise details the ambivalence and engagement of writers with the problems raised by New Deal politics. He notes how state/corporate sponsored writers started to identify with their subjects, seeing themselves as "literary sharecroppers" who were similarly compromised within a system run for business profit. Agee writes in his "intermission" that "a good artist is a deadly enemy of society; and the most dangerous thing that can happen to an enemy, no matter how cynical, is to become a beneficiary" (*FM*, 355). Szalay thus notes the logic of this compromise where *Famous Men* "is in the end a book; Agee is in the end a capitalist" despite his radical aims.[9]

One way of explaining these contradictions is to view *Famous Men*, as Szalay does, in the context of contemporary debates over political and literary experiments, showing the conflicts and ambivalence embodied in the text as symptomatic of wider conflicts in the era over the aims and effects of both literary and political experimentation. Indeed, *Famous Men* clearly displays the tension between progress and conservatism, laissez-faire and planning, optimism and pessimism, the individual and the collective that were central issues of the era.[10] Yet, by locating the political and aesthetic inheritance of the text and viewing it within the historical moment of its conception, we can also see that *Famous Men* reflects more closely the fight over words and their function in the 1930s. In its concern with the printed word as a (failed) means of communication, *Famous Men* thus attempts a practical experiment with language theories that were central to avant-garde politics in the early twentieth century, as well as critical debates since. In *Famous Men*, Agee attempts to create a new medium of expression that would put into practice Ezra Pound's demand for a new aesthetic based on logopoeia (i.e., the creation of a new language based on the stimulation of the receiver's mind by the simultaneous expression of the image of an object—phanopoeia—with an aurally induced emotional correlation—melopoeia) (Pound, *ABC of Reading*, 32). Throughout writing *Famous Men*, Agee developed a similar theory of expression based on "four planes," the dynamic interaction between experience, expression, reception, and meaning. Agee's interest in the visual and the rhythmic as a politics of expression is thus both a continuation of modernist experimentation with the politics of language, and the desire to free the subject through a language revolution, and a response to poverty, photography, and mass culture in the 1930s.

To begin excavating Agee's textual politics, it is important first to look at the way Agee became disenchanted with the political experiments of the early part of the decade, notably the New Deal. Just out of a literature degree at Harvard, he began working for *Fortune* magazine the year that Roosevelt was elected. The first article that brought him to the attention of the editors at *Fortune* was a report about the New Deal's most ambitious project; the creation of the Tennessee Valley Authority (abbreviated as TVA in the following) to ensure regeneration of a vast area of the Southeast. Providing raw materials both "good and ill," the South was a "laboratory for a great experiment," he noted, and the TVA "prepares to fashion a civilization which, in a certain important way, is new and significant to all the U.S." The civilization promised by this experiment was truly an American utopia; "a decentralization of industry, regional planning on a large scale, a well-wrought and well-controlled balance between the Jeffersonian dream of an agrarian democracy and the best characteristics of what so many people like to call the Power Age."[11] Like the New Deal itself, this experiment was also a social experiment in human culture, where those "forgotten men," such as the South's isolated and illiterate farmers, many of whom seemed to belong to a premodern era, "must be raised and reconciled" to higher standards of living without losing their "Americanism," "All of which is very fine. It has an epic quality—and a quality more easily put into words than in deeds" (Agee, The Project, 90). Agee would return to the problematic ease of these words (and their failure to effect "deeds") time and again over the next few years.

The TVA project appeared to herald and create a new phase in American history, one in which Americans were taught how to live in what popular economist Stuart Chase called the "economy of abundance." Published in 1932, Chase's *A New Deal* argued the necessity for more control over the economy by government to reduce the risks of random capitalist economics. To Chase free market economics had led to a new illiteracy: "the ignorance of the consumer, in the face of high pressure salesmanship."[12] Unable to read beneath the superficial sign—the words of the advertisement—the consumer in the 1930s was, to Chase, a new illiterate. Agee's comments on middle-class illiteracy in his section on education in *Famous Men* echoed this sense that despite being formally educated few understood the meaning of the signs surrounding them: "few doctors of philosophy are literate, that is, that few of them have the remotest idea how to read, how to say what they mean, or what they mean in the first place, the word literacy means very little even as it is ordinarily used" (*FM*, 306). The bad use of language was most evident in advertising. Having penned advertising copy himself, Agee was well aware of the way language could delude. To Chase, advertising represented a system of waste and degeneracy that underlay an unplanned and uncontrolled economy, provoking "fantastic distribution costs, cross-hauling, excess capacity, a lopsided industrial development, due to the relative ease of high-pressuring novelties as against necessities and honest comforts" (Chase, *A New Deal*, 232–33). *Fortune*, however, appeared to respond commercially to the New Deal plan for remembering the forgotten man and balancing rural with industrial: "what's good for a run-down system is good for a run-down sales plan" and to "nail down a vital part of your market." "We must balance our menu for selling…and do some substantial country-style thinking for selling families living on farms," argued an ad for promotional space in *Successful Farming* that accompanied Agee's article.[13]

To Agee, however, consumer illiteracy and ignorance may have been more apparent in the contrast between the consumer fantasies and the realities faced by the rural poor than in the inability of consumers to consume functionally. Throughout the period he worked for *Fortune*, advertisements for homes and consumer objects peppered the magazine that were directly in opposition to the used and worn-down, cheap and homemade objects that Agee describes in so much detail. *Famous Men* parodies and undercuts the consumer paradigms of both *Fortune* and the New Deal, revealing the discourse of inequality that lay beneath the advertisements repeatedly shown in the magazine. In contrast to the ideas of structural control, houses and structures described by Agee in *Famous Men* are a precarious balance of chance and order, of construction and deconstruction, where the Gudger's farm is compared to a "water spider" sustained "upon the blind breadth and steady heave of nature" (*FM*, 129). No such contingency affects the homeowner reading *Fortune*: a house and its structure were rationally composed: "Engage an architect now and build at the bottom of the market" argued one advert, with an image of man sitting on the steps of a huge colonial style pile.[14] Plush residences could be beautified and protected as "A high, attractive Anchor Chain Link Fence keeps tennis balls on the court and the unprivileged players off."[15] In *Fortune*, progress was defined by a machine-like functionalism that linked economic to social efficiency through consumption. In an article of October 1935, architectural progress was represented by the ultramodern functionalist house built by architects such as Richard Mandel, a style of architecture which reconstructed "[Americans'] shelter in terms of workability" and efficiency. The photographs accompanying the article examined the modern house in its constituent parts with headings such as "The Front Porch," "The Den," "The Cellar Stairs," "The Bar," "The Kitchen," that appear ironically paralleled in Agee's own dissection of the structure and contents of the tenant farmer's house.[16] To Agee, the structures dominating the lives of the sharecroppers were "attempting their own symmetries, yet not in perfect line...caught between the pulls of nature and science" (*FM*, 146). His description of these structures parallels his understanding of the contingency and power relations of literary and language structures. Agee presents an alternative to the corporate modernism in *Fortune*; a deconstruction of the structure that exists outside of commodity relations "created of economic need, of local availability, and of local-primitive tradition: and in their purity they are the exclusive property and privilege of the people at the bottom of that world" (*FM*, 203). Ownership comes not from purchase but from the creative reappropriation of capitalist detritus.

If these structures represented precarious language systems then their contents also represented signifying units in a shifting semantic system. Again, capitalist fantasies are deconstructed through the comparison of the contents of homes in *Fortune* with their diminished counterparts in *Famous Men*. Cutlery, in *Fortune* advertisements, "achieves startling beauty by its symmetry of line," which defies obsolescence and decay; "Today, continental is a modern. Tomorrow it will be a tradition."[17] Yet in *Famous Men* cutlery is unplanned, random, and encased, not in a presentation box or on display, or in "correct table setting" laid out "European style," but tucked behind a piece of wood tacked to the wall, minimal, fragmented, and asymmetrical. "[T]he forks and knives and spoons are of that very cheap, light, and dull metal which seems to be almost universal among working-class families, and in the more charitable and idealistic kinds of institutions, and which impart to every ounce of food they touch their peculiar taste and stench, which is a little like that of a can which has contained strong fish." The forks and knives can only be understood through a variety of signifying systems: through taste, history, position, and class. Nothing matches, Agee notes, no two "plates, or cups, or glasses, or saucers, are of the same size or pattern" (*FM*, 181).

Agee thus parodies the commodity fetishism and *planned* obsolescence found in *Fortune*'s ads, where you may "decide you need *a fresh deal in silver*—or an added supply—because 'when you entertain, your service fails to stretch into the generous array of matched beauties you'd like to see.'"[18] Agee thus exposes the consumerist aesthetic for both its exclusivity and its inability to represent a shifting, contingent, reality. A New Deal, "a fresh deal in silver" (or a fresh shuffle of the same set of cards) here becomes little more than a revision of the commodity within the same old game.

**Figure 4.1**  Walker Evans, "Kitchen Wall in Bud Field's House, Hale County, Alabama, 1936"
*Source:* Courtesy of Library of Congress, Prints and Photographs Division, FSA-OWI Collection [Reproduction number: LC-USF342-008144-A].

Indeed, by 1935, New Deal reforms appeared to have reached a watershed, where spending increasingly substituted for structural reform.[19] The aims of the TVA also shifted from an experiment in regional planning toward the corporate production of power and fertilizer (Schlesinger, *Age of Roosevelt*, 386). Agee's disillusion with *Fortune* ran parallel to his increasing disillusion over the chimerical relationship between corporate capitalism and the New Deal. In sum, both relied increasingly on "selling" things and ideas to Americans in much the same way. The opposition between New Deal and corporate reform appeared to vanish beneath the similar language both used, and the writer, as propagandist for both, was complicit in aestheticizing this system. Words such as "progress' and "democracy" appeared hollowed of meaning and representative of the political immobility of the system:

as Agee looks at his "helpless" car, stuck in mud near the Gudger's farm, he sees it as "a new dealer, a country dietician, and editor of Fortune, or an article in the New Republic" (*FM*, 372). The static, useless, language of these reformers and capitalists—aligned here—appeared stuck to Agee. All are the same; all are going nowhere.

By the time Agee was on his way South to record the lives of sharecroppers for *Fortune*, a balanced "utopia" still seemed far from realization. Indeed, the failure of the New Deal to help the farmers was apparent in the way he met them: turned away from work relief because they were, technically at least, not unemployed. Not unemployed by word, or on paper, but unemployed in "deed." New Deal methods to save agriculture had been shown to be of no "substantial benefit to the southern tenant," as Edwin Embree stated in *Survey Graphic* in March 1936. The New Deal's Agricultural Adjustment Administration had only increased the hardship of the tenants and despite its abolition by the Supreme Court, "each patching up of the existing order seems to be used to depress a little further this dependent group."[20]

Because many New Deal economists saw underconsumption of mass-produced goods as a significant cause of the Depression, the need to increase the purchasing power of the Southern poor as a way of relieving poverty became a target of both business and government policy. Tenancy and rural poverty in the South became a matter of intense focus in the mid-1930s, for without the expanded purchasing power of the Southern states the economic balance between production and consumption on a national basis appeared stymied. The importance of consumption in the South was confirmed in 1938 when the National Emergency Committee's *Report on Economic Conditions in the South* declared "The South is the Nation's greatest untapped market and the market in which American business can expand most easily."[21]

To Agee the problems facing America would not be solved by creating new consumer literacy, advertising to the poor, or selling consumer goods to tenants on the farms that he visited in Alabama in 1936. To Agee, the idea of taking the superficiality of *Fortune*'s consumerist vision into the lives of sharecroppers was as much a monstrosity as was "spying" on them. Much of *Famous Men* attempts to illustrate the New Deal's dearth of political vision through the contrast of the corporate/consumerist vision with the object, and abject, reality he describes. Agee criticizes the corporate liberal dream of social progress through the redistribution of consumer goods in his "Two Songs on the Economy of Abundance" published in 1936. "Watch well The Poor in this late hour / Before the wretched wonder stop: /Who march among a thundershower / And never touch a drop."[22] By this point Agee's experience at *Fortune* and his disillusion with conventional reform politics led him to see the answer in aesthetic experimentation rather than social reorganization. This was not a retreat from politics, however, but an art that "addressed the health of the social whole" (Augsburger, *Economy of Abundant Beauty*, 174) and a key social and political task of the writer. Freeing up the words and language from common misperceptions and misuse, creating a new liberatory aesthetic that reconnected words with their real (albeit situated and temporary) meanings was, to Agee, also freeing the man. In his essay published that year in *New Masses*, "Art for What's Sake," Agee argued that experimental artists were radicals because "any new light on anything, if the light has integrity, is a revolution" (as quoted in *Economy of Abundant Beauty*, 174). Spurning experimental art, Agee warned, led to art "thereby skimped of certain glandular secretions whose deficiency can impair force, clarity, and even size of reach: to say nothing of richness, subtlety, variety, comprehensiveness, discovery, total accuracy, total courage, total honesty, and a few other qualities which art can use all it can get of." The revolutionary potential of newness and experimentation "is important whether it frees the Scottsboro boys or not" because it can communicate "the materials of dreams and the fluid subconscious, irrationalism, the electrically intense perception and representation of 'real' 'materials' " (as quoted in *Economy of Abundant Beauty*, 174). Contradicting the idea that the experimental led solely to solipsism, Agee argues that rather than being a retreat from the political and the real, experimental texts fundamentally enable political and social change. How could language, especially "radical" experimental language, appear a political solution to the problems of the South? To Agee and some of his contemporaries, language that failed to communicate effectively was certainly central to the political stasis in which the New Deal appeared stuck. Reform politics, as Augsberger notes, "depended heavily on representation and synecdoche...[and] required the simplification and the rhetorical power created when a single comprehensible image replaced a complex, ambiguous reality" (*Economy of Abundant Beauty*, 180). As Agee had discovered in his TVA article, words were easier than action and yet when words were confused with reality (i.e., when they were used ideologically in place of action) they became part of a huge deceit. His disillusion with words and the failings of the New Deal in the South are summarized in his ironic use of Roosevelt's statement "You are farmers; I am a farmer myself," which illustrated the inability of language to express reality and the way politics could use words to delude and trick (*FM*, 111). Sick of political rhetoric and the misappropriation of language, among his "Plans for Work: October 1937," Agee wrote of his intention to work on a dictionary of key words, where certain words, "Love, God, Honor, Loyalty, Beauty, Law, Justice, Duty, Good, Evil, Truth, Reality, Sacrifice, Self, Pain, Life, etc. etc. etc." would be "examined skeptically in every discernable shade of their meaning and use."[23] At the same time he intended to write an "Anti-Communist Manifesto" that would show the "misconceptions, corruptions, misuses, the damage done" in contemporary communist writing and action. In addition, he intended to work on a project about "miscommunication; the corruption of ideas" making "Analyses of the concentricities of misunderstanding, misconditioning, psychological and social lag, etc., through which every first-rate idea and most discoveries of fact, move and become degraded and misused against their own ends" (Agee, *Collected Short Prose*, 140, 147). His section on education in *Famous Men* clearly illustrates such instances of miscommunications, misconditionings, and degradations: "*The Open Door:* open to whom"; "*Stories and Games*: both, modified by a school word, and in a school context"; and "*Trips to Take.* Trips indeed, for children who will never again travel as much as in their daily bus trips to and from the school" (*FM*, 300). The cumulative effect of this education is not useful information or joyful discovery but a series of "afflictions, bafflements, and half-legible insults" that leave the children with "no equipment to handle an abstract idea" (*FM*, 299, 313).

Taught that these words were a form of "truth," the Gudgers were essentially victimized through a series of lies and miscommunications. Agee's belief that new forms of expression and new types of art were "of central importance...to the good of the human race" (*FM*, 232) came from his knowledge of the multitude of language reform texts produced in the interwar years. All these systems of language reform and experimentation—from Esperanto through to the Futurist's "words in liberty" and Neurath's visual Isotypes—varied in every way, apart from their utopian goal of improving the human condition. Cultural production in the first half of the century had taken on a new impetus arising from ideas about the future of literature and communication, with those such as Ezra Pound, I. A. Richards, C. K. Ogden, and Rudolph Carnap calling for new ways of understanding and representing the language and landscape of modernity.[24] At the same time many educators and writers argued for a new politics of reception, a new practice of reading. Agee saw the importance of both a new form of writing and reception: "That [language] should have and impart the deftness, keenness, immediacy, speed and subtlety of the 'reality' it tries to reproduce, would require incredible strength and trained skill on the part of the handler, and would perhaps also require an audience, or the illusion of an audience, equally well trained in catching what is thrown" (*FM*, 236). Modernist poet Ezra Pound also focused on the importance of the reader in the process of creating meaning. To him, "[a]ny general statement is like a cheque drawn on a bank. Its value depends on what is there to meet it" (Pound, *ABC of Reading*, 25).[25] Writers, educators, and philosophers argued the necessity of a new type of reader, one who could respond to the new understanding of linguistic relativity that emerged out of the discoveries of De Saussure, as well as Einstein.[26] Responding to this new understanding of the relationship between science, language, and revolution, Ezra Pound suggested that "the proper METHOD for studying poetry and good letters is the method of contemporary biologists" (*ABC of Reading*, 122). Likewise, Agee argued for a new relativistic expression, where "the importance and dignity of actuality and the attempt to reproduce and analyze the actual" was central to his mission to communicate in a new, more effective, and scientific way: "an art and a way of seeing existence based...on an intersection of astronomical physics, geology, biology and (including psychology) anthropology" (*FM*, 245).

Despite this, Augsberger convincingly argues that Agee's experimentalism comes out of his rejection of reform politics, a politics that relies on the use of representative and synecdochal language. Although this is a valid way of reading Agee's political stance, his belief in language reform can also be connected with the pragmatism of early New Deal thought. After publishing *The Economy of Abundance* in 1934, New Deal economist Stuart Chase also switched to language reform in a book entirely about language titled *The Tyranny of Words* (1938). As a New Deal pragmatist and as a writer of social and economic tracts, Chase saw the inability of language to effect change (or praxis) as a serious problem that needed to be addressed on an intellectual and social level. This was to be done through a popular new understanding of language as something mobile, relative, and situated, and by the elimination of meaningless archaisms and timeworn language patterns and habits. This would mean a radical break with the past, which would in turn infuse language with new potency and agency.[27] "Confusions persist and increase," Chase argued, "because we have no true picture of the world outside, and so cannot talk to one another about how to stop them. Again and again I come back to the image of the map. How can we arrive at a given destination by following a grossly inaccurate map, especially when each adventurer has a map with different inaccuracies?" (*Tyranny of Words*, 352).

In many respects, *Famous Men* is an aesthetic response to the call for a new pragmatic use of language, one that has social use and continues to envision reality as something in constant flux, as polysemous and fluid. Seeing words as the key to political and social progress, Chase wrote *The Tyranny of Words* in an attempt to popularize the difficult concepts coming out of science and linguistics in the early part of the twentieth century; central to his book was the work of naturalized Polish American Alfred Korzybski—inventor of the system of General Semantics—and the work of British pioneers of the Basic English Movement, C. K. Ogden and I. A. Richards.[28] Korzybski's system of General Semantics illustrated how miscommunication happened by exploring how words worked within structures to compose meaning. Korzybski explained that there were three classes of signs or labels for things; first, those which named common objects (cat, dog, hat); second, those identifying clusters and collections of things (mankind, the white race); and third, terms referring to essences and qualities (freedom, truth, individualism). To Chase the goal of General Semantics was "find the referent," for "When people agree on the thing to which their words refer, minds meet. The communication line is cleared" (*Tyranny of Words*, 9). To Chase, understanding Korzybski, Ogden, and Richards, could help prevent the two major sins of language: identifying words with things and misuse of abstract words such as "liberty, justice, and democracy." This was important for ease of communication and, as I. A. Richards wrote in *How to Read a Page* (1943), utilizing new forms of communication could prevent tyranny and war.[29] In *Famous Men*, Agee was also in continual search for the referent, revealing the thing "as the thing is": the important thing to remember "about Gudger is that he is actual, he is living, at this instant. He is not some artist's or journalist's or propagandist's invention: he is a human being" (*FM*, 209, 240). The semantic and philosophical investigations of I. A. Richards were highly important to Agee's work. He was taught by him at Harvard, and Richards continued to influence Agee's understanding of words. Robert Fitzgerald describes in his memoir of Agee how Richards developed his and Agee's understanding of the complicated construction of reality as it emerged through language: "Richards would put three X's on the blackboard . . . to represent poem, referent and reader, suggesting that a complete account of the poem could no more exclude one X than another, nor the relationship between them. Nor were the X's stable, but variable. *Veritas* had become tragically complicated."[30] To Agee, "Words, could, I believe be made to do or to tell anything within human conceit . . . But it must be added of words that they are the most inevitably inaccurate of all mediums of record and communication, and that they come at many of the things which they alone can do by such a Rube Goldberg articulation of frauds, compromises, artful dodges and tenth removes as would fatten any other art into apoplexy" (*FM*, 236).

Agee's central concern with language and communication in many ways offers an aesthetic parallel to Chase's study, which argues for a practical application of the ideas of linguistic structuralism and semanticism as tools for enabling economic justice, peace, and sanity in a world that appeared to have lost meaning by the end of the 1930s. As Chase summarized, "First a war that killed thirty million human beings. Then a speculative boom, which, after producing more bad language to sell more fantastic propositions than in the entire previous history of finance, exploded like the airship Hindenburg. Finally, when a little headway has been made against the economic disaster, the peoples of Europe, more civilized than any other living group, prepare solemnly and deliberately to blow one another to molecules" (*Tyranny of Words*, 351). The effects of poor use of language were apparent—he argued—in war, poverty, and unemployment. To Agee, words had also become corrupted by becoming generic terms emptied of any meaningful use: the word "sharecropper" could not even be used in any meaningful way as "it has very swiftly, and within very few years, absorbed every corruptive odor of inverted snobbery, Marxian, journalistic, jewish and liberal logomachia, emotional blackmail, negrophilia, belated transference, penis-envy, gynecological flurry and fairly good will which the several hundred thousand least habitable and scrupulous minds of this peculiarly psychotic quarter of the continent can supply to it" (*FM*, 455).

Experimentation that would overthrow traditional language patterns and the empty use of words and rhetoric would enable a new, less obscuring and less oppressive map upon which a new reality could be based. Agee views this attempt to remap reality in a very different way to documentary realists and journalists of the time, and this is perhaps why his attempt has often led to contradictory readings of both his aesthetic and his politics. What was most important to both Chase and Agee was locating the reality beneath the word, and to do this "[y]ou abjure all metaphor, symbol, selection and above all, of course, all temptation to invent, as obstructive, false, artistic" (*FM*, 235). This representation of reality is not a "naturalism" or "realism" of a documentary nature, and neither is it a fixed reality, but to Agee it must reflect the reality as it is situated in time, space, and memory. Agee's text thus explores the approach by which meaning might be returned to words through a simultaneous communication of various temporal and spatial existences of the word/object on a variety of planes.

To both Agee and Korsybski's system of General Semantics, the true meaning of the word is in the result/effect—what a man does with it—and not what he says or writes about it. This underlies the performative and multilayered, even ambivalent (or contradictory), quality of Agee's text.[31] As in pragmatism, the meaning lies in the resultant effect/action not in the thought or the word alone. Meaning then, is always relativistic, situated within certain structures but always changing and connected closely with other conditions of transmission and reception. For Chase, "the meaning of an event is not something fixed and eternal, but shifts with the context or the operation which is being performed on it" (*Tyranny of Words*, 34). To reproduce the complexity of this continually changing structure, Agee utilizes the idea that there are "four planes" or methods of communicating: "To get my own sort of truth," he explains, "I must handle it from four planes: That of recall; or reception, contemplation, in *media res*"; "As it happened": "By recall and memory from the present" and "As I try to write it." "All of these are 'in strong conflict,'" he asserts (*FM*, 235). To Agee, structures (both houses and language) exist only in temporary and contingent relationship to their constituent parts and the landscape in which they are situated. Further to that, more "planes" operate once you try to recall or remember a thing or an event, and further still when you try to write it, and even further when it is read/received. Hence, the possibility of failure during this transmission process appears quite overwhelming and causes Agee to continually revisit the processes and attempt to repeat them. Agee's struggle to describe physical structures in *Famous Men* can thus be seen on another level as a struggle to present the new structures of meaning in a highly complex linguistic environment.

In Korsybski's case, he invented a model called the Structural Differential to represent his similar theory of the structural situatedness of language (a theory which took impetus from anthropological studies of the cultural context of language and studies of "primitive" peoples and translations), which he used to demonstrate his theories of language and semantic transmission. Just as Agee's "four planes" the Structural Differential is the basis by which reality can be perceived. The three-dimensional model illustrated varying levels of the abstracting process by which meaning was obtained from objects. In exposing the various levels by which meaning is constructed, Korzybski attempted to make the processes of understanding and communication clear. Similarly, to Agee, exposing his method of creating meaning by describing his "four planes" and exposing the structural situatedness of the language and art he produced, he attempted to clear the semantic "block," to eliminate false art and false meaning on the page.[32]

As Agee exposes the realities behind the words printed in *Fortune,* the language of corporate fakery is uncovered and ideally destroyed. If nothing else, Agee illustrates the variety of abstractions that create the corporate idea of "progress." Yet, because he cannot remove the meanings or contexts of the corporate abstractions, which are preexisting in his text, any more than he can remove the commercial detritus in the tenant's house, *Famous Men* becomes a palimpsest in which the words of the corporate and bureaucratic orders are over-written with a new system of communication. Not only is this evident in the obvious reuse of seemingly "neutral" adver-tisements and sales communications, but in the disorganized organization of the book's structure as a whole. Like all of the reports in *Fortune* and the social studies published in the era, *Famous Men* appears to divide its content into logical and discrete sections that will address separate issues. "Money," "Shelter," "Clothing," "Education," "Work" (for comparison *The Report on Economic Conditions of the South* also had sec-tions on "Education," "Health," "Housing," "Labor," etc.). *Famous Men,* however, refuses to stick to the rigid boundaries and apparent scientific logic of these descriptions, continually circling other ideas, introducing breaks and digressions, or picking up the thread elsewhere. Refusing to close the topic, Agee illustrates that no matter how logical or rational the lan-guage appears there is always a different, contingent, reality behind it, and that reality is in a state of constant change.

The importance of exposing or showing the structure of expression and understanding on "four planes" thus becomes a political act of showing how language operates ineffec-tively and how it can be manipulated to control and delude. *Famous Men* thus exposes a variety of narrative conventions and linguistic explorations in ways that have led it to be confused with more familiar genres (e.g., Marxist realism). But rather than being an attempt to create a new "successful" or universal narrative—one that resolves all linguistic and structural tensions—it ends up as an exploration of narrative and linguistic failure in the late 1930s: "The communication is not by any means so simple. It seems to me now that to contrive techniques appropriate to it in the first place, and capable of planting it cleanly in others, in the second, could be a matter of years, and I shall probably try none of it or little, and that very tortured and diluted, at present" (*FM*, 12). The problem of communicating meaning through words, Agee shows, is far from solved through books or texts. They all end up entangled within the capitalist/commercial nexus, appropriated for tyrannical use by their circulation in the capitalist semantic order. "As a matter of fact, nothing I might write could make any difference whatever. It would only be a 'book' at best," he concludes (*FM*, 13).

Showing the variety of planes on which the structures exist, Agee illustrates the complex operation of representation, which ultimately dooms him to failure: "Trying, let us say, to represent, to reproduce, a certain city street...Your medium, unfortunately, is not a still or moving camera, but is words...and what have you in the end but...the opposite pole from your intentions, from what you have seen, from the fact itself" (*FM*, 235). By the end of the 1930s, the utopian aims for language and politics undoubtedly appeared lost or failed as Europe entered into a meaningless war based on the political abstractions of "democracy," "freedom," and "fascism." As Agee noted, "[W]ords like all else are limited by certain laws" (*FM*, 236). It should be no surprise then that Agee retreats somewhat from written language into his fascination with visual forms of expression after the publication of *Famous Men*, retreating into the "Universal Language" of film and away from the difficulties of written truth.[33] Indeed, even before *Famous Men*, Agee views the camera and the visual as purer forms of expression than words.

Yet, even those forms of representation have their expressive limits, he noted in a notebook entry in 1935, and in the end only music had the truly lyric scope that he wished for in literature; "Can words spoken or written possibly break through it again, break through and get free" (Fitzgerald, *Remembering Agee*, 64). The optimistic attempt to free words mired in the semantic mud of modern corporate control in *Famous Men* leads to an excursion into a lost (or never reached) past of linguistic utopianism and becomes in the end a warning of the consequences of a failed political experiment. Looking for resolution, Agee beseeches "let us then hope better of our children, and of our children's children; let us know, let us *know* there is a cure, there is to be an end to it, whose beginnings are long begun, and in slow agonies and all deceptions clearing" (*FM*, 399). Yet it is not to be: as readers we are denied an end or an easy answer, such comfort is illusive. In the last section, "On the Porch 3," communication has become aural and abstract, temporary and unfixed, sublime, sexual, but ultimately not human: as he and Walker Evans lie on the porch they listen to the animal sounds of two foxes calling to each other in the night, and Agee experiences the "frightening joy of hearing the world talk to itself, and the grief of incommunicability." Yet, his grief is assuaged by the "small yet absolute comfort of knowing that communication of such a thing is not only beyond possibility but irrelevant" and that even though such communication appears an impossibility "I do not relinquish the ultimately hopeless effort with entire grief: simply because that effort would be, above most efforts, so useless" (*FM*, 470). Agee, perhaps, may have agreed with Chase that "Good language will not save mankind. But seeing the things behind the names will help us to understand the structure of the world we live in. Good language will help us to communicate with each other about the realities of our environment, where now we speak darkly, in alien tongues" (*Tyranny of Words*, 361).

*Famous Men* may end in darkness, in alien noises and human silence, but it is a silence where words are replaced by a new form of communication: "But now in this structure of special exaltation [talking] was, though not unpleasant, thoroughly unnecessary." It is thus that Agee urges the reader to keep searching for better ways of communicating, even in the face of failure, for as he commented in his journal, "perhaps more can be communicated through describing the problems of communication and its technology, than through the direct attempt."[34]

## NOTES

1. Eugene Zolas, "Workshop," in *Imagining Language: An Anthology*, ed. Jed Rasula and Steve McCaffrey (Cambridge, MA: MIT Press, 1998), 42.
2. Stuart Chase, *The Tyranny of Words* (New York: Harcourt, Brace, 1938), 18.
3. Quotes taken from two separate texts by Ezra Pound.
   *ABC of Reading* (London: New Directions, 1987 [1934]), 32.
   *Machine Art and Other Writings: The Lost Thought of the Italian Years*, edited and introduced by Maria Luisa Ardizzone (Durham, NC: Duke University Press, 1996), 122.
4. James Agee and Walker Evans, *Let Us Now Praise Famous Men* (New York: Ballantine Books, 1974), 266. All subsequent references are to this edition and are located within the text.
5. Michael Augsburger, *An Economy of Abundant Beauty: Fortune Magazine and Depression America* (Ithaca, NY: Cornell University Press, 2004), 156. The full quote is as follows: "The cost of the 'radical' artist's opposition to the symbol-creating artists of the Popular Front, the New Deal, and corporate Liberalism was a withdrawal from political discourse."
6. William Todd Schultz, "Off-Stage Voices in James *Agee's Let Us Now Praise Famous Men*: Reportage as Covert Autobiography." In *American Imago*, 56:1 (1999), 101.
7. For discussions of the relationship between writers and politics in this era see: Alan Felreis, *Modernism from Right to Left: Wallace Stevens, the Thirties and Literary Radicalism* (Cambridge: Cambridge University Press, 1994); Paul Gorman, *Left Intellectuals and Popular Culture in Twentieth-Century America* (Chapel Hill: University of North Carolina Press, 1996); Richard H. Pells,

*Radical Visions and American Dreams: Culture and Social Thought in the Depression Years* (New York: Harper and Row, 1973); Michael E. Staub, *Voices of Persuasion: The Politics of Representation in 1930s America* (Cambridge: Cambridge University Press, 1994).

8. James S. Miller, "Inventing the 'Found' Object: Artifactuality, Folk History, and the Rise of Capitalist Ethnography in 1930s America," *Journal of American Folklore* 117 (466), 373.

9. Michael Szalay, *New Deal Modernism: American Literature and the Invention of the Welfare State* (Durham, NC: Duke University Press, 2000), 27.

10. Martin Rubin, "The Crowd, the Collective and the Chorus: Busby Berkeley and the New Deal," in *Movies and Mass Culture*, ed. John Belton (London: Athlone, 1996), 50–92. See also Michael Denning, *The Cultural Front: The Laboring of American Culture in the Twentieth Century* (London: Verso, 1996); and Barbara Melosh, *Engendering Culture: Manhood and Womanhood in the New Deal Public Art and Theater* (Washington DC: Smithsonian, 1991).

11. James Agee, "The Project Is Important," in *Fortune*, October 1933, 88.

12. Like the TVA, however, the New Deal was from the start a compromise with industry, a "third road...the drastic and progressive revision of the economic structure avoiding an utter break with the past." Stuart Chase, *A New Deal* (New York: Macmillan, 1932), 173.

13. Advertisement for Successful Farming, *Fortune*, October 1933, 98.

14. Advertisement for *The Architectural Forum*, *Fortune*, October 1933, 146.

15. Advertisement for Anchor Fences, *Fortune*, October 1933, 178.

16. "The House that Works," *Fortune*, October 1935, 63.

17. Advertisement for International Sterling, *Fortune*, October 1935, 1.

18. Advertisement for International Sterling, *Fortune*, January 1935, 1. A similar comparison could be made between Agee's section on hats and an article titled "$200,000,000 Worth of Hats," in *Fortune*, January 1935, 50.

19. Arthur M.Schlesinger, *The Age of Roosevelt: The Politics of Upheaval* (Boston: Houghton Mifflin, 1960), 386.

20. Edwin Embree, "Southern Farm Tenency: The Way Out of Its Evils," in *Survey Graphic: Magazine of Social Interpretation*, 25:3 March, 1936, 149.
21. David L. Carlton and Peter A. Coclanis, eds., *Confronting Southern Poverty in the Great Depression: The Report on Economic Conditions of the South with Related Documents* (New York: St. Martin's Press, 1996), 78.
22. James Agee, "Two Songs on the Economy of Abundance," in *The Collected Poem of James Agee*, ed., and with an introduction by Robert Fitzgerald (London: Calder and Boyars, 1972), 58. See also Augsburger, *An Economy of Abundant Beauty*, 155.
23. *The Collected Short Prose of James Agee*, edited by Robert Fitzgerald (London: Calder and Boyars, 1972), 137. Agee cites I. A. Richards as the inspiration for his dictionary. Eugene Zolas's "transition's Revolution Word Dictionary" (1929) with a list of "words to be retired from active service . . . democracy, republicanism, liberalism, and humanism," may also have been influential. See Jed Rasula and Steve McCaffery, eds., *Imagining Language: An Anthology* (Cambridge, MA: MIT Press, 1998), 27.
24. As Marjory Perloff illustrates, the first radical experiments with new ideas of perception, the visual, and the construction of meaning in literature and art, came early in the twentieth century. See, Marjory Perloff, *The Futurist Movement: Avant-Garde, Avant-Guerre, and the Language of Rupture* (Chicago: University of Chicago Press, 1986); and John White, *Literary Futurism: Aspects of the First Avant-Garde* (Oxford: Clarendon, 1990).
25. See also Todd Avery and Patrick Brantlinger, "Reading and Modernism: 'Mind Hungers' common and uncommon" in *A Concise Companion to Modernism*, ed. David Bradshaw (London: Blackwell, 2002), 243–262.
26. Ronald W.Clark, *Einstein: Life and Times* (New York: Avon Books, 1972), 118.
27. The phrase "tyranny of words" is also central to the "Manifesto of the Futurist Painters" (1910). http://www.unknown.nu/futurism/painters.html
28. Chase also claimed to be influenced to a lesser extent by Lancelot Hogben, Ludwig Wittgenstein, Charles Beard, and Friedrick Von Schiller.

29. I. A. Richards, *How to Read a Page: A Course in Effective Reading with an Introduction to a Hundred Great Words* (London: Routledge, 161), 241.
30. Robert Fitzgerald, "A Memoir" in *Remembering Agee* ed. David Madden (Baton Rouge: Louisiana State University, 1974), 59.
31. According to Szalay, Agee's aesthetics of performance "makes him more like a sharecropper than a landowner" given that New Deal art, intrinsically performative, becomes a form of labor rather than a commodity (Szalay, *New Deal Modernism*, 27).
32. Alfred Korzybski, *Science and Sanity: An Introduction to Non-Aristotelian Systems and General Semantics* (Lakeville, Connecticut: International Non-Aristotelian Library, 1933).
33. Miriam Hansen, "Universal Language and Democratic Culture: Myths of Origin in Early American Cinema," in *Myth and Enlightenment in American Literature*, ed. Dieter Meindl and Friedrich W. Horlacher (Erlangen: Universitatsbund Erlangen-Nurnberg, 1985), 321–51.
34. Michael A. Lofaro and Hugh Davis, eds., *James Agee Rediscovered: The Journals of* Let Us Now Praise Famous Men *and Other New Manuscripts* (Knoxville: University of Tennessee Press, 2005), 124.

# 5

# AGEE, EVANS, AND THE THERAPEUTIC DOCUMENT: NARRATIVE NEUROSIS IN THE FUNCTION OF ART

## *Paul Hansom*

If the evolution of civilization has such a far-reaching similarity with the development of an individual, and if the same methods are employed in both, would not the diagnosis be justified that many systems of civilization—or epochs of it, possibly even the whole of humanity—have become neurotic under the pressure of civilizing trends?[1]

—Sigmund Freud

[A]ny attempt to achieve a vicarious immortality through the creation of culture leads to a neurotic obsession with the past and the future.[2]

—Norman O. Brown

*Let Us Now Praise Famous Men* is a neurotic book, a phenomenological discourse on being emerging out of such overwhelming self doubt it illustrates (albeit in complicated fashion) the impossibility of guaranteeing the very self as a being-in-time. In fact, its existential crux leaves us wondering what we can actually point to, to suggest we exist at all.[3] It makes me nervous just to think about it. This chapter emerges from the conundrums of writing the "self" into existence, of viewing the "past" in the present, and the impossibility of escaping the disturbing traps of "nostalgic modernism."[4] Underpinning much of my logic here are Freud's speculations that culture and cultural production are inherently neurotic activities, emerging as they do from the terrors of existence and the desire to escape death; that "art," in all its many guises, is the transference object for this anxiety, producing formal structures through which we, in turn, experience and understand the time flow of our own lives. My understanding of the neurotic, however, is closer to the American analytical model developed by Karen Horney rather than Freud's, since seeing the individual condition as a socially dynamic category is more useful for my purposes than a strictly psychosexual persona. Although sexuality is certainly a dynamic engine in its own right, modernity produces such enormous anxiety with its incessant psychotic demands that the neurotic is clearly a *social* type and not a private individual. Neurosis is an ideology, a way of perceiving the world. And it is this neurotic condition *Famous Men* mirrors so effectively, structuring not only the verbal-visual interplay of the text, but also our own readerly engagement with it.

"James Agee"
"who the hell am I, who in Jesus' name am I?" (*FM*, 384)

First, the easy part—easy because Agee is a self-dramatist, reveling in the violent tugs of his own anxiety, wearing the self-conscious struggle on his metonymic sleeve. Agee is desperate to reclaim and preserve a historic sense of his identity to fix himself and his literary task in the world of action and concrete gesture, to give himself a real presence in writing. Thus, his own anxiety structures the struggle within the text, whereby he paradoxically tries to free himself from the burden of his own past while raveling himself up within that very history. Agee is a classic neurotic seeking to rationalize his neurosis, providing the facts of his anxiety by controlling its narrative shape, by bringing it into being in, as, and through his own text. Rather than occupying the textual porch, think of Agee as reclining on the therapeutic couch, constructing a perpetual present to stave of his death anxiety in which the parameters of his ego/I control the representational structures giving them concrete shape. *Famous Men* is literally a self-conscious text exploring consciousness of the self, while also occupying a particular moment in the perceived time-continuum, where self-construction hungrily attempts to guarantee now, existence, and being. As a result, Agee is a haunted man, spooked by the myths of transparency and objectivity, which lie frustratingly beyond his representational power.

Agee recasts perceived external experience around his consciously unstable ego, and while the tenant farmers are fascinating epiphenomena, they loom incidental to the self and its celebratory power standing at the center of the narrative, exploring the subject of and through his own consciousness. The farmers are a pretext to the insistence that Agee is *there*, a continual insistence reinforcing the anxious recognition that he might actually be nothing more than a textual echo. But, of course, there is no secret about this since he sees the whole venture as "a reproduction and analysis of personal experience, including the phases and problems of memory and recall and revisitation and the problems of writing and communication" (*FM*, xvii).

Such an ambitious project is inevitably doomed to "successful failure" because the work-in-process directly parallels the writerly persona as a similar work-in-progress, its outlines inimically linked to the shape of his own personality. In this way, the governing narrative principle of this dramatization is "Agee's own encompassing (not simply observing) consciousness, itself the center as well as the surrounding medium of the subject."[5] Just as Evans's photographs, Agee's neurotic self-consciousness utilizes the subjects and context as means for self-exploration, relying on the continual "sonority of being" that provides the paradox of the text/self as completed in some concrete way.[6] Similarly, while Evans's photographs conjure up the particular through a fleeting visuality, so Agee's text offers the sudden fragment of consciousness through a complex performance of insistence and disavowal, you see it but you do not, it is there and but it is not there. By providing an illusory, imaginative empiricism, the text suggests the language of the writing subject is a spiritual resonance, a hieroglyph of being, lying beyond categorization—but which can be experienced on the page—as it were.

By avoiding any conscious borrowing from traditional narrative genres—he seeks to create a new form—Agee insists on the particular collisions of experience to make meaning. Inevitably, it is an anticollision relying, as it does, on the simultaneous structuring of the ego and the literary project. The narrative design outlines neurotic cultural drives and most of the text is dominated by the "On the Porch" section—an implicit nod to the anthropological "writing-up period,"—which centralizes the self at the moment of contemplation and creation in pseudoobjective reverie, a site that playfully manipulates the familiar and the uncanny. Here, Agee patterns his notion of culture through an instrumental design that places himself as superobserver and unsure commemorator. By turning the porch into a self-conscious raft, Agee explains and utilizes the self-reflective literary strategy, manufacturing statements such as "Why make this book, and set it at large, and by what right, and for what purpose, and to what good end, or none," and "I'll do what little I can in writing. Only it will be very little. I'm not capable of it; and if I were, you would not go near it at all. For if you did, you would hardly bear to live" (*FM*, 9, 13). Agee is central yet self-effacing, inadequate but closer to some mysterious spiritual transcendence, and it is from this design that Agee develops his own transcendental mythos by universalizing the single experience through "miniature thinking" (Bachelard *Poetics of Space*, 150), conjuring the world into an expression of his authorial self to possess it: all the world is Agee. Ultimately, of course, this in itself is a contradiction of space and transcendence, the adventure itself impossible as Agee attempts to make himself more than what he is, or can be. Agee's narrative authenticates "himself" as emanation and nothing more, casting external History into the personal sphere, into an *auto-history*, thus straining "towards a complete and coherent expression of his entire destiny."[7] Agee wants everything in the world and of himself, but his construction is limited, rendering that world into a series of psychic artifacts, suggesting the impossibility of things ever being outside of consciousness, of experience, of ever being representable in an accurate way. In a key sense, *Famous Men* becomes a therapeutic gesture, attempting to provide stability in language even while these efforts are caught in contradiction. Out of this stressed relationship, "we share our form and our life with the perceived objects: we become, in our creative act, all the objects we behold, and, more importantly, the order of those objects" (Olney, *Autobiography: Essays*, 33). Thus they become monuments of the self at the moment of composition, monuments which are a mainstay against death and nonbeing. And this we understand and unconsciously accept in our moment of reading cognition.

The text is a drive on Agee's part "to make their lives bespeak and symbolize *his*, to condense himself into the conditions of their existence and so actualize himself along with them" (Taylor, *Chapters of Experience*, 70). While the text is, in Agee's words, "a *book* only by necessity," it is fraught with the contradictions surrounding the recording self, where the "governing instrument—which is also one of the centers of the subject—is individual, anti-authoritative human consciousness" (*FM*, xlviii, xlvi). The construction of monuments implies a fear of the transience of the past, that remembrance may not occur, that the self will simply vanish. This hungry wanting engulfs the whole past, transforming it into nostalgia, a place where the self can reflect on time's changes, safely evoke our own transience and the knowledge that death is immanent. To see Agee's prose as "historic" is actually correct, because the embodiment of his yearning self is a specific historical accretion, a residue. And while he does not help us create the past in any "accurate way," he *embodies* the past and a moment of thought, a process attempting to hold the present before it was lost.

From the porch all meaning flows, because Agee resides there, it provides him with the necessary vantage. Yet by being on the porch he is the outside insider (a spy) stealing vital information while passing for a trusted individual. It is no surprise that this section is also the beginning of Agee's active strategic *remembrance*, in which the self comes to occupy the central position of writer/recorder. "We lay on the front porch" (*FM*, 21) is the prefiguring of a cinematic flashback, where we meet the characters of Agee and Evans even before the narrative begins proper. Thus, Agee intervenes to construct his own omnipotence, celebrating the "truth" of his own vision.

Similarly, in the section titled "AT THE FORKS," Agee gets the opportunity to study his behavior while constructing it: "We backed slowly,... and I got slowly out and walked back toward them, watching them quietly and carefully, and preparing my demeanors and my words for the two hundredth time" (*FM*, 32). After scaring the black couple while trying to get details, Agee concludes, "They made us, in spite of our knowledge and our own meanings, ashamed and insecure in our wish to break into and possess their church" (*FM*, 39–40). In trying to understand their evaluation of himself, the text appears objective to Agee's subjective posturing. In an extremely egocentric section that revolves around the artistic consciousness, the text explores the problems of communication and the difficulties in developing trust. Agee is still an outsider, regardless, and it is this position that gives him a narrative vantage point.

Exploring the difficulties of getting in, or fitting in, becomes an obsession for Agee because it signifies the need to be accepted into this alien world, by recognizing that it is totally alien and somehow lying beyond his representational skills. What for other writers is a question of procedure, for Agee, creates the way he understands his material and his own specific textual character. This self-presentation is evident in "A COUNTRY LETTER" (*FM*, 47): "And it is in these terms I would tell you, at all leisure, and in all detail, whatever there is to tell: of where I am; of what I perceive"

(*FM*, 52). Strategically, the letter moves from first encounters to inner sanctum, where Agee (the I, here) perceives, selects, and describes. Clearly the letter is addressed to us, following a mode that is creative, stylized, and ultimately gives presence to the personal. Agee wants to present it all and/through himself to us, not as an abstraction, but as a "felt" existential intensity in which the self is central to the fabric of textual experience.

But the stream halts when Agee inserts a "COLON: CURTAIN SPEECH" (*FM*, 97), which literally punctuates the text as a whole. The action stops and Agee steps forward to address the reader with his doubts about continuing: "But there must be an end to this: a sharp end and clean silence: a steep and most serious withdrawal: a new and more succinct beginning.... For one who sets himself to look at all earnestly, at all in purpose toward truth, into the living eyes of a human life: what is it there beholds that so freezes and abashes his ambitious heart?" (*FM*, 99). What indeed? Agee must stop at the uncertainty of his own aesthetic practice and description of his writerly self, because he is unsure of what he is, or even what he is trying to do: "for I must say to you, this is not a work of art or of entertainment, nor will I assume the obligations of the artist or entertainer, but is a human effort which must require human co-operation" (*FM*, 101). At best, all he can fall back on is common ground, which we should be skeptical of accepting since he presents himself as a "cold-laboring spy" (*FM*, 134). Yet textual spies do have a tendency to be double-agents, and in the creation of his character he successfully creates a self-serving other: "If I were not here; and I am alien; a bodiless eye; this would never have existence in human perception" (*FM*, 187). His observation and narrative enshrine a personalized history within the text. Real existence is turned into mythic/poetic flight and description in which "life" is necessarily co-opted by art.

Following the doubting panic of the colon address, Agee falls back on a series of notes, which function as platforms (porches?) of qualification, justifying his own aesthetic methodology. Here he sets himself against the "reformer" and

those interested in "questions" to insist that details are vital
to human significance. But which ones, and how to guarantee
their impact, is difficult to ascertain. Agee's narrative must
inevitably talk around objects, describing them, burdening
them with likeness dependent upon choice, while trying to
avoid all "metaphor, symbol, selection" (*FM*, 235). In this he
fails, as he realizes with reference to Gudger, the objective
sharecropper:

> George Gudger is a man, et cetera. But obviously, in the effort
> to tell of him (by example) as truthfully as I can, I am limited.
> I know him only so far as I know him, and only in those terms
> in which I know him; and all of that depends as finally on who
> I am as on who he is.
>
> I am confident of being able to get a certain form of the truth
> about him *only if* I am as faithful as possible to Gudger as I
> know him. (*FM*, 239)

Representation and narrative construction ultimately reflect
Agee's neurotic personality, reinforcing the tendency in the
text to link representation to guilt. The sin of artistic failure is
an obsession with the limits of his own abilities. He is unwor-
thy, he is not God, he cannot control or understand anything
beyond his own words and the limits they instill. In the shocking heart of this neurotic text Agee turns viciously upon himself, damning personal history, art, political revolution, for
what he perceives it to be: irrelevant to the complexities of his
own personality.

   The text is a vast caption to the photographs, promoting a self-consciousness we are meant to adopt, an instabil-
ity we are expected to share. Though the narrative itself may
be "fictional" in the broadest sense, it is, in fact, a concrete
manifestation, which has a truth-emanating form. But what
does it embody? This complicated entanglement plunges
the observer and observed into the experience of historicity
and temporality. What we experience is the flux of neuroses,
the provisional character of personality and the knowledge

that "nothing remembered may remain unchanged."[8] Agee, seeking to escape himself in the name of catholic objectivity, returns to the source of his own consciousness, delineating the patterns of that consciousness, a template of neurotic desperation. And because Agee is anxious he redoubles his efforts to work harder in the old ways, leading him into a dead end where the fractured self and the atomized text reach a zero degree from which all literature never really escapes. In a sense, Agee reaches the bounds of thinkable and representational thought, achieving negative freedom by celebrating both creative potential and the frustrating psychic structures upon which it relies.

"Walker Evans"

"Only I…Only me"[9]

It is possible to develop a coherent approach to Agee's narrative because talking about words is so much easier than forcing language into explaining an image. Evans's photographs are there for all to see, without the metaphoric interference of writing, without the myths of objective representation. Orthodoxy suggests photographs, especially those with a documentary veracity, offer a stability, which needs no justification. The image, as Roland Barthes suggests, "is heavy, motionless, stillborn (which is why society sustains it)"; it has a culturally validating presence. But, as he hints, this solidity is only one side of a continual flux embodying the photographer's own unspoken psychic determinism and the observational time-condition of the audience as well. Ultimately it is " 'myself' which is light, divided, dispersed" and the photograph offers an uncanny certitude to this frantic looseness.[10] Like Agee, "Evans" embodies and represents a struggle to define self-identity in terms of romantic categorization; unlike Agee, however, Evans's neurotic identity is the bedrock of broader institutional discourses that have come to define our conceptions and understanding of modern art. Following Paula Rabinowitz's suggestion that documentaries always have "self-doubts about their status as organs of truth and reality," performing a surprise autopsy on representations of Walker Evans's allows examination of what some of these "doubts" might loosely look like.[11] Evans's rendering of the world photographically provides a material presence, but the general inability to pin-down the "meaning" of his images is concomitant with the inability to pin-down being-in-time. What we are left with are quasireligious appeals to continuity through self (re)presentations and critical discourse. Relying on Evans's iconic status, the photographs are nevertheless remarkable documents of modernist anxiety.

If critical voices smooth the way for aesthetic myths, cultural institutions provide similar functions within the public sphere, providing contexts for locating the work within a broad taxonomy of artistic objects. In 1938, after the successful release of Evans's *American Photographs*, he was given a one-man show at the Museum of Modern Art (itself a very recent experiment in American gift-giving art patronage), thus marking his essential canonization, and the shift of his work into officially proscribed "modern art." As he recognized, "More than I realized it established the documentary style as art photography. For the first time it was influential, you see. The museum is a very influential place."[12] So influential, in fact, that it "confers the identity, the status of artist" (Trachtenberg, *Reading American Photographs*, 239). Under the auspices of John Szarkowski (Director of MOMA), our contemporary notion of "Evans" as modernist became official, a construction giving him the remarkable magical power of creating "the accepted myth of our recent past," of producing a "transcendent documentary photography" in which nothing was imposed on experience, and visual representation was handily turned into truth. Even Evans himself readily accepted this ideological premise, opining dramatically "It's as though there's a wonderful secret in a certain place and I can capture it. Only I, at this moment, can capture it, and only this moment and only me" (*Reading American Photographs*, 56). The secret of art is rendered visible, unlocked by the key-consciousness belonging to the genius of self.

The transcendence of Evans's work above the hack documentary photography produced by Margaret Bourke-White, Dorothea Lange, or most of the iconographers connected with the FSA, must be read as both the development of a modernist aesthetics *and* an indication of its powerful reliance on concrete embodiments of neurosis with its own attendant desire for totalization and closure. In the foreword to *American Photographs* (1938), Lincoln Kirstein claimed "Walker Evans's eye is the poet's eye," a description Evans would never contradict.[13] Nor should Evans, because he saw himself as absolutely "typical as the young Bohemian artist," embodying an antiestablishment attitude: "I think I was photographing against the style of the times, against salon photography, against beauty photography, against art photography...I was a maverick outsider" (*Reading American Photographs*, 237). Evans's own identity is directly connected with this sense of detachment as a necessary part of his creation. As Evans recounts, "I was just in a sense taking advantage of the FSA and using the government job as a chance for a wonderful individual job. I didn't give a damn about the office in Washington—or about the New Deal, really." Similarly, refusing to let his integrity be violated by the corporate shenanigans of Roy Stryker, director of the FSA, Evans insists on his independence: "I've been particularly infuriated by reading here and there that he [Stryker] was 'directing' his photographers. He wasn't directing *me*; I wouldn't let him."[14] In this way the ideal of "personality" is extended not only on individual terms, but also woven into cultural concepts of artistic production. *We* need Evans.

Terrified of contamination by mass culture, terrified by the "homogenization of difference," we hang onto a sense of the self, to rescue it from the realities of our sociopsychic dread.[15] But while Evans's photographs appear to present a motionless (w)hole, a totalizing vision that mythically conjures up the transcendental subject we believe to be the artist-man, these images are also neurotic studies of temporal isolation, totemic fetishes fulfilling the wish-of-art: a fond stability and locating power giving us a point of reference in time. In this way Evans's photographs are religious icons (in the same way that he is sanctified for modernism), acting out an intellectual transfiguration of the profane to the sacred, a dramatization of the clash between the "psychic interiority of living memory and the exteriority of artificial or techno-logical memory."[16]

Evans's images are transformed into contemporary relics invested with an apparently contradictory medieval desire to give the photograph a supernaturalism, making the random significant (meaning-filled), seeking closure on time and space, thereby locating a specific photograph-taking self. This magical guarantee of Evans's presence provides us, the viewer, with a temporary salvation from disintegration and death. Inevitably, the camera reflects a state of being in time and history, and "Evans" as text embodies a myth of contact and presence. His concentration on profane objects and their mundane emanations elevates them to the sacred, where they become extraordinary objects capable of generat-ing reverence. In this sense, they confer eternity not only on the objects photographed, but also on Evans, on ourselves, and human-time in general. This mystical spirit is not only a staple of academic discourse surrounding Evans, but also a staple of photographic analysis in general. William Stott's canonical *Documentary Expression and Thirties America* claims Evans seeks "normal human realities, but ones that have taken a form of such elegance that they speak beyond their immediate existence"; he does not expose reality like a tawdry propagandist, rather "he lets it reveal itself"; and in seeking human realities he finds those that "speak beyond their immediate existence" (Stott, *Documentary Expression*, 269). Invested with a stunning godlike power, Evans also captures all of lived historical experience as we know it, offer-ing a "way of seeing which has appeared persistently through-out the American past."[17]

This religious-photographic sense effectively destroys the past, erasing it in favor of the perpetual contemporary experience, a rapture in the personal realm providing a concrete rendering of the neurotic yearning for eternal life. In the same instant, it transforms historical knowledge into an extreme personalization, where time-past is ineffably linked to self-time. This sickness, this dream place of nostalgia makes the viewer aware of the past *as* the past taking place in the perceivable *now*, in a neurotically displaced denial of the future. The experience of the past-in-the-present means we must consciously construct the past as "history," a deliberate therapeutic fiction stemming directly from present needs. This imposition of ordering patterns on the past provides a fictional guarantee, furthering "the purposes of continuity of identity by reassuring the now self that it is 'as it was then': deserving, qualified, and fully capable of surmounting the fears and uncertainties that lie ahead."[18] Like transcendental ideals, nostalgia too is redemptive, saving history for sentimental contemplation by imposing narratives on the past, which effectively guarantee *us*.

Evans's photo selection at the beginning of *Famous Men* effectively stands on its own, mixing images of buildings, objects, families, juxtaposing the personal with the architectural to give concentrated focus on structural and formal aesthetics. Unlike other photo essays of the period, there is no essential story here, no attempt to provide narratives of the South, of Dust Bowl migrations, or African American folk-digests. Rather, obviously, they are records of what *he* was looking at, gestures toward enshrining a point of view designed to encapsulate an instant of time. The fact that the photographs have no legends or titles to assist in externalized authentication means we face the images without a context other than the point of view offered. Evans removes the photographs from a topical study and places them into an exclusive and "pure" context that uses accuracy (and the verifying presence of consciousness) as an aesthetic device. In this way the subjects are freed from their historical and local references

and are decontextualized yet reassembled into a separate collectivity directed by Evans's personal modernist and neurotic
vision. In short, the image series becomes a collection of aesthetic objects, "liberated from contingency and circumstance
into a space of pure contemplation."[19] Although they are recognizable documentary images, their separation from a historical context, from a factual base, renders them as fetishes
to the notion of the self and reduces the world to a series of
unique, personal viewpoints. Categories of the social specimen become spaces and schemes for the individualizing consciousness, which insists that Evans "sees" better than we do,
that he has access to a truth.

By misunderstanding our relationship to the present as a
transhistorical one, we fail to see that "such use of time almost
invariably is made for the purpose of distancing those who are
observed from the Time of the observer."[20] By separating time
in such a fashion, the moment occupied by the sharecroppers
is used in an ideological and political sense. It serves to reproduce the artistic self, to maintain categories of transcendent
art, and the cozy visual periodization of history. Evans's neurotic photographs insist that in our looking, history can only
be real if we feel it and appreciate it, insisting on the private
time of the viewing self. By chronicling the moment in *Famous
men* (1936, though it was actually published in 1941) "subsequent images of the decade" were not only controlled, they
extended a sense of neurotic time over external material/historical time.[21] Evans's aesthetic conception effectively merges
neurotic desire into a "vision" of what history looks like, in an
activity that melds the personal with external nonego materiality. Within modernity an artist constructs a private, modifiable past out of a transient present to encapsulate the self and
the world and the history of both.

Neurotic art under modernity presents, as Lewis Mumford
puts it, "not self examination but self exposure; not tortured confession but easy open candor; not the proud soul
wrapped in his cloak, pacing the lonely beach at midnight,
but the matter-of-fact soul, naked, exposed to the sun on the

beach at noonday, one of a crowd of naked people."[22] Despite Mumford's purple romanticism here, he does register the problem of art, artist, and ego in the age of mechanical reproduction and the problems of vindicating the narcissistic: as a category or term, the artist has almost no meaning because we all have the artist-ego, everything is already an aesthetic object because everything ratifies the all-consuming ego. The personal becomes a site of narcissistic fascination and history exists as self-gratification, as self-understanding, ultimately becoming egocentric, selfishly organizing what we notice and recall, thereby determining the field of referentiality. *Famous Men* is an important book precisely because it dramatizes a critical cultural moment in which the neurotic individual is invested with artistic power, in which the empirical ideal of the factual world is replaced with the self-as-fact and the self as arbiter of all experience. In this way, the neurotic is naturalized as the contemporary social type, and modernity proves itself to be the beginning of an accelerated individualism familiar to all us postmodernists.

## NOTES

1. Sigmund Freud, *Civilization and Its Discontents* ([1930] New York: Norton, 1989). Quoted in Brown, *Life against Death*, 11.
2. Brown, Norman O. *Life against Death: The Psychoanalytical Meaning of History* (Middleton, CT: Wesleyan University Press, 1972), xi.
3. James Agee and Walker Evans, *Let Us Now Praise Famous Men* ([1941] Boston: Houghton Mifflin, 1988). All subsequent references are to this edition and are located within the text.
4. Michael Kammen, *Mystic Chords of Memory: The Transformation of Tradition in American Culture* (New York: Knopf, 1991), 300.
5. Gordon O. Taylor, *Chapters of Experience: Studies in Twentieth Century American Autobiography* (New York: St. Martin's Press, 1983), 69.
6. Gaston Bachelard, *The Poetics of Space* (New York: Orion Press, 1964), xii.

7. James Olney, *Autobiography: Essays Theoretical and Critical* (Princeton, NJ: Princeton University Press, 1980), 35.

8. Dagmar Barnouw, *Critical Realism: History, Photography, and the Work of Siegfried Kracauer* (Baltimore: Johns Hopkins University Press, 1994), 57.

9. Evans in Alan Trachtenberg, *Reading American Photographs: Images as History, Mathew Brady to Walker Evans* (New York: Hill and Wang, 1989), 56. All subsequent references are to this edition and are located within the text.

10. Roland Barthes, *Camera Lucida* (New York: Noonday Press, 1981), 26.

11. Paula Rabinowitz, *They Must Be Represented: The Politics of Documentary* (London: Verso, 1994), 23.

12. Evans in Trachtenberg, *Reading American Photographs*, 238.

13. Lincoln Kirstein in Walker Evans, *American Photographs* (New York: Doubleday, 1938), 2.

14. Evans in William Stott, *Documentary Expression and Thirties America* ([1973] Chicago: Chicago University Press, 1986), 281. All subsequent references are to this edition and are located within the text.

15. Andreas Huyssen, *After the Great Divide: Modernism, Mass Culture, Postmodernism* (Bloomington: Indiana University Press, 1986), vii.

16. Nancy West, *Kodak and the Lens of Nostalgia* (Charlottesville: Virginia University Press, 2000), xii.

17. Thomas W. Southall, *Of Time and Place: Walker Evans and William Christenberry* (San Francisco: Friends of Photography, 1990) 195.

18. Fred Davis, *Yearning for Yesterday: A Sociology of Nostalgia* (New York: Free Press, 1979), 39.

19. W. J. T. Mitchell, *Iconology: Image, Text, Ideology* (Chicago: Chicago University Press, 1986), 294.

20. Johannes Fabien, *Time and the Other: How Anthropology Makes Its Object* (New York: Columbia University Press, 1983), 25.

21. David Peeler, *Hope Among Us Yet: Social Criticism and Social Solace in Depression America* (Athens: Georgia University Press, 1987), 101.

22. Lewis Mumford, *Interpretations and Forecasts: 1922–1972* (New York: Harcourt Brace, 1979), 243.

# 6

# "Two Prickes":
# The Colon as Practice

*Paula Rabinowitz*


All over Alabama, the lamps are out. So it begins—if that is really what you can call it after dozens of photographs and pages of verse and prose have already accumulated around this famous gesture. An opening, a beginning that inaugurates itself through closure, the day is shutting down—"the house had now descended"—and the two men, the "two prickes,"[1] (*We lay on the front porch:*

This partial parenthetical remark, an opening, a branching forth, italicized so at once hidden behind the enclosure of the left parenthesis, but forcing itself as an emphasis then drifting off into the forking path pried by the colon from which flows nothing but blank space tells us much of what we need to know about Agee's design for his contribution to this book: incompletion, repetition, redundancy, and emptiness. As sleep descends, the dream commences. Date: July 1936. Place: Alabama. Visible scars: "dreaming, that woman, that id, the lower American continent, lies spread before heaven in her wealth [...] still:"[2] Agee has already abased himself, not once, but three times, earlier that Sunday morning. Wrenching fear, shame, and hatred from the eyes of the impoverished white and black tenant farmers he meets on their porch, at their church, in their yard. All these sacred zones already uncovered, disclosed as zones of dispossession, where those who dwell within them barely get by, leave as few traces of their footsteps as possible so as not to incur the wrath of those who have more than they, or who might try to take what little they do have— bodily integrity, self-respect, and native dignity. Agee knows it all, sees it all, and lets us in on his painful self-awareness. It is what disarms us again and again in this maddening book. He always gets there first, undercutting any contempt we may feel for him and his self-regard.

"Performance, in which the whole fate and terror rests, is another matter" (16), declares Agee of his project—to be as Beethoven, to remake affect and intellect so that anyone who crosses this threshold will never know unhappiness again: because dazzling, the composer has transformed the inner wirings of the psyche. You are committed. Agee's contempt for the notion of commitment stems from his sense that to commit an act one must always foresee its many consequences. For the practice of writing is a commitment to the process of unwriting, erasing the text preceding the next outburst by way of his gaps, his parentheses, his sustained phrasing, such as long jazz riffs or his favored metaphor, a fugue, fork- ing and turning and revising and restating until the endless limbs of the sentence, paragraph, chapter, book dissolve the wan commitment of surety and replace it with commitment to the praxis of thought and belief (for this is, as all Agee's most personal work is, a holy text). He is prying open his brain, dis- solving and remaking the synapses—electroshock therapy was introduced in 1937—and if we go along, if we following his forking paths, ours will be reformed too. He writes to Father Flye, and signs his letters "Rufus," in the midst of working on " the book": "I feel as I were disintegrating and 'growing up,' whatever that means, simultaneously, and that there is a race or bloody grappling going on between the two in my head and solar plexus."[3]

The performance—this race or grappling—is staged for a number of different audiences. Contemporary readers (who appeared doubtful to Agee) and those subsequent readers who might discover this oddball work—he was reading Kafka, *The*

*Castle*, a few weeks before traveling South with Walker Evans to begin working on what would become *Let Us Now Praise Famous Men*, whom he called "a great though limited reputation in Europe as one of not more than 3 writers of the century; book spoken of as a contemporary *Pilgrim's Progess*" (Flye 92)—but in the interlude, the "curtain speech" he points to those about whom this book is written and who very likely will never be among its readers. "Colon" describes a methodology as it addresses directly the three tenant families at the "heart, nerve and center of each of these, is an individual human life" (101). The address to those he is about to violate through words as he translates the objects of their lives into thousands of words is a plea and a forestalling of failure that whatever excuses he may make, his act is one of desecration even as it is also an act of love. The colon is sign for Agee, already glimpsed in his Yale Younger Poet's award-winning volume *Permit Me Voyage*, of death and of God. It is how you convey reverence and displace finality while demonstrating difference—the space between living and death. "Dedication" begins to those "who died in honor; and chiefly to these: Christ: Dante: Mozart: Shakspere [*sic*]: Bach: Homer: Beethoven: Swift: the fathers of Holy Scripture: Shelley: Brahms: Rembrandt: Keats: Cézanne: Gluck: Schubert: Lawrence: Van Gogh: and to an unknown sculptor of China, for his god's head."[4] Robert Fitzgerald describes Agee's grasp of Elizabethan and Jacobean poets and their deep knowledge of Latin, "whose rhetoric and metric he made, for a short time, his own" (*Poems* xiii). Both friend and editor of volumes of Agee's poetry and prose, Fitzgerald recognized that prose became the medium most suited to Agee's textual musicality, derived from "the sustained and various shaping of movement in time," and his fascination with "the visual world. [...] A living prosody for him would govern the timing of camera shots, the speed and grain and hue of images, the cutting of sequences" (xv–xvi). But in the early poems, Fitzgerald discerned efforts to cull a grammar, a system of prosody that would textually replicate the movements in time and space of music and cinema. But a living prosody, needed to outline death: In the 1937 poem, "In Memory of My Father," published in *transition*, Agee returns to the colon to convey the spaces death creates within memory. Back from traveling with Evans through Hale County, Alabama, his comments about the "middle south" often turn on his familiarity with its "gesture, landscape, costume, air, action, mystery" (449) sparked by his concentrated return South after more than ten years in New England and New York. Listening to the lowing of a bullfrog, the poem breaks apart; its speaker is brought into the fractured spaces of memory that rearrange conventional punctuation and word spacing extending some words to isolate them, enjambing others to crowd them.

> effortless air : love in the neat leaves the neat leaves : gentle
> colony in your green harbor throes of a common dream
>     throes in
> the leaves, and quiet : sweet tended field, now meditate your
> children , child , in your smokesweet quilt , joy in your
>     dreams, (73)

The poems ends with father and mother reunited as flesh and earth before ascending into light; it anticipates Agee's repeated returns to the events and memories surrounding his father's death in later works: "Knoxville: Summer 1915," *The Morning Watch*, and *A Death in the Family*.

But enough.

As a student of Latin at Philips Exeter, Agee surely knew of the etymological connections between the colon as mark of punctuation and as Roman term for a peasant bound to the land. The colon is a limb or a member (from Greek); but this seems to be a mistake in transcription as colon is first food or meat; then the gut or bowels, the portion of the large intestine that extends from the kidneys to the rectum. It is at once sustenance and shit. And I cannot help but think that Agee treasured this branching out from eating to shitting to fucking.[5] It is a column or a file (from Latin). The army marching across the land to conquer and the conquered tillers of the soil ever vanquished. In all these senses, the colon is doubled and reversed, refuting itself, contradicting and mirroring its meanings. The "two prickes" are at once less than and more than—a shorter pause than a period; a longer one than a comma—a sentence completed with still more tagged on. Complete but needing a supplement:

> The supplement adds itself, it is a surplus, a plenitude enriching another plenitude, the *fullest measure* presence. It cumulates and accumulates presence. It is thus that art *technè*, image, representation, convention, etc., come as supplements to nature and are rich with this entire cumulating function. [...] But the supplement supplements. It adds only to replace. It intervenes or insinuates itself *in-the-place-of*; if it fills, it is as if one fills a void. If it represents and makes an image, it is by the anterior default of a presence. Compensatory [*suppléant*] and vicarious, the supplement is an adjunct, a subaltern instance which *takes-(the)-place* [*tient-lieu*]. As substitute, it is not simply added to the positivity of a presence, it produces no relief, its place is assigned in the structure by the mark of an emptiness. Somewhere, something can be filled up *of itself*, can accomplish itself, only by allowing itself to be filled through sign and proxy. The sign is always the supplement of the thing itself.[6]

Jacques Derrida's explication of the role of the supplement as both theme and system in a chain of supplements is another way of describing différance, the movement between presence and absence "Until death." Agee's desire to find a method and means to convey the themes of his excursion into a "portion of unimagined existence" begin with the colon, with this mark that cuts the sentence in two, this double mark that splits open the structure of the sentence as it sutures one limb onto another.

But, of course, it does not quite divide the sentence—or at least not evenly. Agee's recourse to the colon was a gesture recognizing the extensions to a sentence that the colon allows. "Others say, a colon is to be used when the sense is perfect, but the sentence not concluded."[7] By the time Agee inserts his section entitled "Colon," the sense is perfect, but the sentence is far from over. To complete it, one must endure. There is something of the waiting out of a jail term embedded in this dodge. This forestalling of the end pushes prose along, leads inevitably to more. Agee's "Colon" comes at the end of what has been the long prelude to the book's detailed observations of objects, clothing, shelter, and work. He has "moved in" on the Gudgers entering their household, appropriating their speech, imagining their innermost thoughts.[8] He has sat next to Emma (his sister's name);[9] suffering with her as she is driven with deep dread to meet her new husband; he has heard Annie Mae wonder (*How was it we were caught?*) (91); he has stood around the sawmill awkwardly joining men: "chopping, sawing, snaking, hauling, the shearing surface shriek of the saw: and it is not thirty-two minutes past six, and among these men are George Gudger and—" (95).

This conclusion to "Part One: A Country Letter" leaves us hanging in suspension as we are meant to fill in the blank space with Agee's name, or with our own or with any of the two billion then alive on planet earth. Part One ends with a rarely used dash, returned to toward the end of this long curtain speech. And becomes necessary again in the final "On the Porch: 3" symphony, long after "the last words of this book have been spoken" (441) and we enter, along with the two resting men, a sonic immersion into the deep silent sounds of the country, a chorus of foxes calling across the night. "It ran eight identical notes to a call or stanza, a little faster than allegretto, in this rhythm and accent:

——— :—: -—: " (464)

This baying, sublinguistic, is the musical answer to Annie Mae's imagined soliloquy voiced nearly four hundred pages before; "it will be very different) (? :)

( (?) ) :)
How were we caught?" (81).

These marks, indicating sonic rhythms, the anguish of unful-
filled desire, send Agee beyond the sentence and its rules of
grammar. Like the hidden sexuality they belie, these marks
insist on their presence by interrupting prose, charting what
cannot be said, absence.[10] They open the space of the book, as
the colon opens the sentence to further revision.

The "Colon" section begins with a direct question posed
to George and by extension, his family: "how am I to speak of
you as 'tenant' 'farmers,' as 'representatives' of your 'class,' as
social integers in a criminal economy, or as individuals, fathers,
wives, sons, daughters, and as my friends and as I 'know' you?"
(100). To answer his own query, Agee traces the evolution of
cells into the complexity of human existence and uses this ever
expanding series of concentric circles—"its structure should be
globular" (101)—as a model for how he will approach the rest
of his task. How alter the dilemma that "one can write only
one word at a time?" The lineality of writing risks destroy-
ing the globularity of "human life," risks seeming to be "lists
and inventories merely, things dead unto themselves, devoid
of mutual magnetisms" (111). But Agee has already collapsed
his structure into an ever tightening list of degradations as
he hurries through his litany of the childhood, adolescence,
marriage, work, that will make up the life of one "southern
alabamian tenant farmer" (107), this colon:[11] "the constant
lack of money, need, leanness, backbroken work, knowledge of
being cheated, helplessness to protest or order this otherwise,
clothes worn, landlords imposed on one, towns traded in—"
(110). Agee breaks off here, as he had a few pages before in the
midst of detailing the grinding labor required to eke out one's
sustenance under this "criminal economy."

Instead of continuing his iteration of what, by the time he
was writing and certainly by the time the book was published,
had become a massive cliché, he interrupts himself. Postponing
the end through "example, explanation or elaboration," the
sentence of hard labor and, ultimately, death within a criminal economy is delayed, deferred, pushed off into a distant
future.[12] "This is all one colon:" he declares, but to what does

"this" refer? All that has come before, all that will come after, or the fifteen pages between his two long dashes, both broken-off sentences, where language fails in the face of physical labor, of the brutalized body of an undernourished, poor man at work, performing dangerous and dull tasks simply to provide a bare existence for himself and his family. Agee's interruption, his momentary awareness of Gudger's presence, functions as the colon in elocution: it "Stops the Voice...privately."[13] Agee cannot continue his list; but he cannot stop either. So the rest of the book is limb, prosthesis, and extension. "I" ventriloquizes her (Annie Mae), then addresses "you" (George), then betrays and is ashamed, even if he is not "caught" by them, or precisely because he is not caught, and so must confess, circling round in just the same obsessive way Rufus catches his mother fondling her rosary after the father's terrible accident in *A Death in the Family*.

The rosary beads advance yet go nowhere, like an endless film loop. And the colon marks the page, advancing the sentence and the book, as the sprocket holes assure that the film will work its way through the projector at a regular speed. *A Death in the Family* begins with Rufus and his father Jay taking an illicit trip to a Chaplin picture at the Majestic and later to a saloon, despite his mother's disapproval. The two sit together through the second part of a William S. Hart western, then watch the Chaplin short, and stay through the Western until they "came in, but they watched him kill the man all over again; then they walked out."[14] Agee narrates the misadventures of Charlie's tramp almost frame by frame, sequencing the images to mimic the experience of film viewing: a boy and his father together in that strange collective intimacy of the darkened theater. In his foreword to *Let Us Now Praise Famous Men*, "James Agee in 1936," Walker Evans calls the "first passage of A Country Letter...particularly night-permeated" (xi). A darkness that is shared by the two, two men, set off together, not really alone, as they are living within the close quarters of a family of six, but still alone, as a boy and his father escaped from the proper household that

a white middle-class Southern woman kept in 1915 into the
crowd of a darkened movie house.

The colon is queer. Two prickes—member and rectum,
or at least the column ending at the rectum and the limb
that branches out from the trunk. Agee's prose, forking and
branching as it does with its endless digressions and repetitions, moves toward the stillness of two men quietly listening
to two foxes calling through the dark; these two men entering
the home of another, rifling his belongings, moving his furniture and clothing to set up the best composition, fingering
the objects left trustingly about in baskets and chests. Before
unveiling the house, Agee as always unveils himself, revealing a
sweet memory permeated with the self-loathing of a "sensitive
boy" masturbating.[15] Agee's only volume of poetry, *Permit Me
Voyage* (1934) nods to Hart Crane's six poems *Voyages*, written for his lover Emil Opffer, just as the beginning invocation
of Chaplin "the God of his boyhood,"[16] in *A Death in the
Family* recalls Crane's great poem "Chaplinesque." Crane, like
Whitman, had refashioned American poetry into a kind of long
scansion collecting the objects jettisoned around the harbor
and its city. Theirs is a poetry that seeks out and speaks of the
body, the pleasures of the male body and homosexual desire.
Crane's long poem, *The Bridge*, was published the same year
Evans's first volume of photographs came out from Liveright.
Good friends since the 1920s, Lincoln Kirstein suggested that
knowing Crane as he was writing *The Bridge* prepared Evans
for his collaboration with Agee, "whose verse, springing at
once from Catholic liturgy, moving pictures, music and spoken language, is our purest diction since Eliot."[17]

The collaboration between the two men, as Zoe Trodd
points out, is more elusive than that found in the other phototextual books against which Agee was writing and Evans
was photographing.[18] Both the layout—separating uncaptioned images from text—and the apparent affect, with
Evans's stark and simple compositions countered by Agee's
wild prose, diverges. Yet, Trodd argues, each artist is working
from a concept of the cinematic—Evans through editing and

montage in the sequencing of the photos, Agee through his "writing in a continuum" (62). And, I would add, the colon is the sign of this process, as sprocket hole, as caesura, as extension. Collaboration suggests a working together; elaboration a working out in detail through to the finished product. The colon is the sign of both, two prickes extending together. No one is off the hook, either—not George and his family or the others; not the readers who with each page are drawn deeper into the work, implicated in the criminal economy detailed in it. This is what Agee means that this is a work of "human effort which must require human co-operation" (111).

Like so many critics, Trodd is only the most recent to be taken in by Evans. She comes close to noticing the "performance" in one of his photographs; she notes the photograph of William Fields holding onto the bed frame with the messed sheets behind him resembling "angel wings." But she misses the far more obvious performances—the rearranged bed in the Burroughs' bedroom, placed not in the stark parallel lines as Agee notes when he and Evans "spy" on the house, but at an oblique angle in order to get it all in the frame; and most glaring, the image of "Lucille Burroughs picking cotton, Hale County, Alabama, Summer 1936," which, since it was shot in July long before cottons bolls appear, is staged in a field full of leafy plants, not the bare branches of a mature plant, to demonstrate what the physical labor of stooping to pick cotton looks like. Collaboration implies complicity; the two are in this together.

And nowhere more so than when the two men take apart the inside of the Gudgers' house, item and by item, describing and photographing with a pained but almost ecstatic abandon. "I shall touch nothing but as I would touch the most delicate wounds, the most dedicated object," remarks Agee. His reverence before the meager stuff held in this house, this "shelter," turns to "shame" as he remembers "his labor, George, at this instant, hard, in the strenuous heat, and upon the tanned surface of this continent, this awful field where cotton is made, infinitesimal, the antlike glistening of the sweated labor of nine million." From the hard, glistening bodies of the millions who work the land, Agee shifts to his most intimate revelation, his "criminal gliding and cold serpent restiveness" of an adolescent slithering through the "large unsentineled home" of his grandfather, methodically fingering and smelling everything room by room, then taking off his clothes to lie upon each bed, masturbating before each mirror: "I permitted nothing to escape the fingering of my senses nor the insulting of the cold reptilian fury of the terror of lone desire which was upon me:" (136–37). Normally interior to the sentence, here the colon breaks open shame and its hot, guilty, pleasure, again making possible the leap from labor to desire, from Gudger's house to his Grandfather's to Hart Crane's Grandmother's attic where her old love letters are cached; the intimate interior.

**Figure 6.1**  Walker Evans, "Home of Cotton Sharecropper Floyd Burroughs." Hale County, Alabama (1935 or 1936)

*Source*: Courtesy of Library of Congress, Prints and Photographs Division, FSA-OWI Collection [Reproduction number: LC-USF342-008128-A]. [www.loc.gov/pnp/fsa/8c52238u.tif].

"[U]pon this house," says Agee, "the whole of heaven is drawn into one lens; and this house itself, in each of its objects, it, too, is one lens" (136).[19] At once focal point and lens, the house mirrors the doubled efforts of Evans and Agee, George's labor and Agee's masturbation. Container and contained, it holds the characters and their lives "squarely in front of us, silent and undefended in the sun" (137). Camera, meaning room in Italian; what is taking the picture and what is being taken. "I am being made witness to matters no human being my see" (136). This strange sentence construction, Agee's voyeurism recast as a transgressive passivity uttered in the passive voice (and I can barely write this without Microsoft Word's eternally vigilant grammar check feature letting me know Agee and I have been breaking the rules), like the colon calls out for more. So we get it: fifty thousand words devoted to the families' "Shelter" to complement the fifteen images.

The house sits almost dead center of the frame in the cropped version of the photograph used in *Let Us Now Praise Famous Men*. It fills the space, balanced above the ground on three or four stones set evenly along the front, the whole balanced between scrubby earth and bleached sky, balanced on the sides by a lean-to and a shed, brushes and trees retreating from each into the background, balanced on the porch by the two girls each dressed in white sitting on either side of their mother and younger brother, balanced further by the two windows placed off-center in the two bare clapboard walls, their horizontal lines framing the open porch, bisected down the middle by five steps leading onto the porch and the long open corridor running through the house. Light and shadow divide the spaces into dark charcoal grays within the space of the porch and underneath it, and bright, almost white, grays on the surfaces of roof and walls. The house appears suspended, the pure form of house, its elements stripped down to the basics: wall, window, roof, and beams. The porch roof upheld by the pine beams provides refuge from the white hot sun; darkness is shelter, too. The house faces the picture of the Gudger's bed, smooth white sheet covered with flies, angled out from the wall beneath the upturned rifle; it follows the first image of the landlord Chester Boles and then the double portraits of George and Annie Mae. As Trodd indicates, a narrative: owner, parents, bed, house, children. But closer inspection of the picture reveals something more—another narrative. For, to the left of one sister is a small boy, her brother, unbalancing the symmetry of the two sisters seated on bent hickory chairs. Receding still further behind Annie Mae bent over as she bites off a thread while sewing is a slender silhouette of Agee himself, foot extended onto Annie Mae's rocker holding it in place, his hands cradling a Brownie camera (its double lens hidden) pointed at Squinchy, caught in motion, in all likelihood responding to Agee's call, "Look at me!" Only Louise, on the right side intently watches the main action—Evans's box camera across the yard. Thus two cameras are simultaneously at work—two shutters closing over two lenses, one outside, the other within, the frame.

Agee's description of the house renders it into another version of the colon: "Two blocks, of two rooms each, one room behind another" (138). Or rather two colons, linked together, as an analogy :: . And there are many already available: The "hard" body of laboring George is to the "cold serpent" of desiring Agee as the "central instrument of our time" (11), Evans's camera, is to Agee's "soft pencil" (49). But enough. The house is defined by "Bareness and space (and spacing)" but these are almost indescribable (155); how can one speak of absence, emptiness, and lack? Yet Agee manages twenty more pages. Lingering, as he had in his Grandfather's vacant house, over each button, fragment of torn magazine page, dish towel carefully placed in chests, on walls, on nails. And before this ten pages on the structure. We have already looked deeply at it, if we have done Evans's pictures justice and pored over them as Agee insists. But now we revisit the structure in words and the reiteration send us on a methodical "balancing of 'monotonies'" (143) in which variations and repetitions of the following words and phrases occur: "two rooms," "exact square," "exact center," "exactly opposite," "left of the house," "right of the house," "dead center," "perfectly symmetrical," "two front walls," "two hollow squares," "two projections," "its short square," "the square boxes," "the square front walls, raised vertical to the earth, and facing us as two squared prows of barge or wooden wings," "vertical boards," "horizontal to the earth," "horizontalities," "horizontal parallels," "pure symmetry," "sternest Doric," "most massive symmetry and simpleness," "a matchless monotony, and in it a matchless variety," "driven according to geometric need," "four chambers upon a soul and center of clean air," "almost perfect symmetries," "this exact symmetry," "horizontal," "parallels," "not quite square," "centers and opposals of such rigid and earnest exactitude," "more powerful than full symmetry," "one of the larger fugues of Bach," "strategic to structure; and regimented by need," "in full symmetry of the sun, " "the balanced masses"(138–46).[20] Boards and nails, shadow and light, conspire to create this Blakean vision of ruthless and defiant sparseness holding out against scarcity and need the possibility of protection and nurture. Parallel lines, Doric columns, verticals and horizontals, these are all aspects of the colon's fierce symmetry. Like the house, the colon, makes a space, encloses it; yet it makes space, opens it.

Almost fifty years earlier, W. E. B. Dubois investigating "the Quest for the Golden Fleece," in Georgia's Black belt, also revealed the squalid living conditions of black tenant farmers and sharecroppers. He found nothing comparable to the classic proportions evident in the Gudger's home.

All over the face of the land is the one-room cabin,—now standing in the shadow of the Big House, now staring at the dusty road, now rising dark and somber amid the green of the cotton-fields. It is nearly always old and bare, built of rough boards, and neither plastered nor ceiled. Light and ventilation are supplied by the single door and by the square hole in the wall with its wooden shutter. There is no glass, porch, or ornamentation without. Within is a fireplace, black and smoky, and usually unsteady with age. A bed or two, a table, a wooden chest, and a few chairs compose the furniture; while a stray show-bill or a newspaper makes up the decorations for the walls. Now and then one may find such a cabin kept scrupulously neat, with merry steaming fire-place and hospitable door; buy the majority are dirty and dilapidated, smelling of eating and sleeping, poorly ventilated, and anything but homes. Above all the cabins are crowded.[21]

By the time Agee was recording his observations about the white tenant farmers' homes, the image of rural privation had entered the popular imagination through mass media magazines, films, and photographs. Agee and Evans were assigned originally by *Fortune* to report on white tenants, precisely because, as Du Bois noticed in 1898, cotton had been moving from the Black Belt to the White Belt, as land gave out and the crop moved West to Texas (though he maintains, at the turn of the century, cotton was still being chiefly cropped by blacks). But primarily because the project was expressly not an examination of the legacy of the "slave *régime*" as Du Bois's essays comprising his book were (Du Bois 84). Agee's and Evans's construction of the Burroughs's house was meant to be seen in opposition to those of the other families' dwellings (and to the even more derelict housing of black and white sharecroppers and tenant farmers seen in Margaret Bourke-White's book *You Have Seen Their Faces*). Theirs was a relatively stabile home—in all senses—while the Fields's and the Tingles' were teetering on the brink of dissolution. Their house, like the colon, was capable of supporting extensions, additions, like the two men, writer and photographer, who stayed with them as boarders during their three week investigation.

Agee's apparently unstructured prose, held together by the ever present architecture of the colon, stands in contrast to the kind of determined symmetry of Du Bois's effort to spell out the conditions of Southern black peasantry two generations before the Depression. Du Bois shapes his magazine pieces into a series of rigid forms, from the repetitive nature of the chapter titles each beginning with "Of" to the quotation of a few lines of poetry and a few bars of music to the introductory and concluding gestures of autobiography to the flights of fiction, memoir, history, economics, and political theory that constitute the core of each chapter. His efforts to scan sound into his prose—through the musical notations beginning each chapter and most powerfully in the final chapter "Of the Sorrow Songs,"—brings the "unmeaning jargon," as Frederick Douglass had called slave spirituals and work songs, into full harmony with his philosophical project of limning modern subjectivity through the experiences of African Americans' "twoness" and "double consciousness."

Where the house of the southern black peasantry Du Bois encounters as a teacher and sociologist were overwhelmingly single room dwellings, even if the consciousness of those living within them were marked by "twoness," Agee and Evans find the houses of the three white tenant families to be larger, rambling structures, though shoddy and dilapidated, for the most part. Only the Burroughs's home withstands scrutiny as it maintains its emphatic control through symmetries, horizontal and vertical. This structural regularity threatens to come apart as each knotty board warps, each nail rusts, each shingle rots. The effort of organizing chaos into a semblance of sustained and certain order, displayed relentlessly through Evans's starkly congruent images of the square house and its eloquently placed contents, is wildly undermined by Agee's aberrant punctuation.

Colon use declined throughout the twentieth century, even as its presence in the titles of scholarly articles in certain humanistic fields increased.[22] One of the most important grammar handbooks from the early twentieth century makes clear that "[g]ood punctuation is desirable for the sake of propriety...the lack of it is uncouth."[23] Among the uncouth aspects of punctuation are the many "bad" usages of the colon, which seems especially misunderstood. However, the authors of the newly revised *Composition and Rhetoric* rather exuberantly declare: "the colon is a mark of anticipation. It is generally preceded by a statement which arouses a feeling of expectancy or anticipation, and is always followed by words or groups of words which satisfy that feeling."[24] These standard handbooks, used at Harvard and various seminaries and exclusive secondary schools, such as St. Andrews and Philips Exeter, were surely referred to by Agee's instructors. Agee himself was prone to noting the etymology of words, as he indicates in a letter to Father Flye about an excised passage from an essay he was writing for *Fortune* on the orchid as commodity. Full of colons, as he delves deeply into his antipathy for the flower, he deploys the punctuation mark as a rhetorical device. "Any flower is built of course for one special purpose: to propagate itself: of any flower, the private parts and the face are one & the same, and that seems more than all right to me: but it does seem to me that the orchid abuses the privilege. 'The orchid gets its name from the Greek *orchis*, which means testicle'" (Flye 81). He plays (so to speak) with the colon, the orchid, the testicle, and the text in this private exchange about a piece of writing meant for publication that will probably not see the light of day.

Agee's excesses oscillate between "uncouth" breaking of the rules and "the expectancy and anticipation" the colon will "satisfy." As he calls attention to the rules of punctuation, both by breaking them and by their exuberant overuse, he recalls the odd heritage of radical punctuation any American writer from the 1930s sensitive to "the people"—as much as Agee distained that word—would recognize: Walt Whitman and his unusual penchant in the 1855 *Leaves of Grass* for using the four-point ellipsis. In his prose poem, "Dedication," collected in *Permit Me Voyage*, Agee moves from his family to his teachers and on "To Mark Twain; to Walt Whitman; to Ring Lardner; to Hart Crane; to Abraham Lincoln; and to my land and to the squatters upon it and to their ways and words in love; and to my country in indifference" (*Poems* 11). Twain, Lincoln, Whitman—even, to an extent, Crane—were among the pantheon of authors celebrated by the literary left.

Whitman, especially, was heralded by literary radicals during the Third Period through the Popular Front. Typical was
Mike Gold's famous 1929 call in the *New Masses* for "A Jack
London or a Walt Whitman," who, as young workers, must
"Write. Your life in mine, mill and farm is deathless signifi-
cance in the history of the world."[25] Of course, Agee loathed
the uncouth revolutionary fervor of Gold's proletarian put-on;
still he was a product of the same left Harvard literary crowd
deeply influenced by Vernon Parrington's monumental study
*Main Currents in American Thought* (1927); Granville Hicks's
*The Great Tradition* (1933); and later F.O. Matthiessen's
*American Renaissance* (1941).

These works traced a massive and continuous stream of
revolutionary populist connections between the people
and the American land, which requires a new form of
expression—including new forms of punctuation—to connect the writer, his (as these greats were almost all male, especially as Emily Dickinson's dashing experiments in prosody
remained unknown because her editors regularized her wild
lines by removing all dashes[26]) folk, their land and country.
Whitman's extended ellipses at once distance and connect
the parts of his long lines, as they set off one type of rough
from another. Like Samuel F. B. Morse's newly invented code
of dots and dashes (whose first transmission across the East
River Whitman reported on for the *Brooklyn Eagle*), these
marks foreground the components of speech. Breaking words
down to letters, then letters themselves into a binary series of
long and short sounds—noted typographically as dots and
dashes—Morse code offered a universal form of communication, yet forced attention to the isolated fragment of each sound,
atomizing phonetics into rhythmic tapping. Communication
across space happened as speech disappeared.

Agee's long rants—including his hysterical list of nouns,
many terribly "uncouth," in the "Note" to section 4 of the
Appendix—distanced him from what he considered the ruling
orthodoxies of both genteel middle-class culture and bohemian literary radicals. His list of words, serving as a verbal

punctuation to the glossary he offers on the term "tenant," declares that language has run away from him—its wild abandon, nouns piling upon nouns, threatens to undo his precise effort to differentiate the term tenant from its more common, though technically inaccurate, sharecropper. Like the excess detailed by the colon, offering us too many choices as sentences branch out and then branch again until they recede even further from the original object or subject, this flood of profanities and icons exhausts language, setting up the final lapse into the silent sounds of deep country night ending this exhausting book.

Receding from the two piercing sets of eyes that have surveyed and absorbed the faces, bodies, clothing, housing, and meager land and possessions of the three families, the night forecloses sight. Nestled close in the dark, the two must finally rest; their long effort to have us know these various beings— them, the families, ourselves—as "the text read continuously, as music is listened to or a film is watched" comes to a close (xv). Deprived of sight, the ear finally takes over, following the baying of the foxes, then the desultory talk of two tired men attending occasionally to the "two masked characters" roaming about, "until at length we too fall asleep" (470–71). A book that begins without words concludes with silence. The long colon linking the first nightfall in Alabama to the last elaborates a broken line of text, extending through the lives of the colons Agee and Evans encounter. At last seeing and listening are over. The book concludes with a period. That is proper. "But there must be an end to this: a sharp end and clean silence: a steep and most serious withdrawal: a new and more succinct beginning:" (99).

( (?) ) :)

## Notes

1. *The Oxford English Dictionary* (London: Oxford University Press, 1961) Volume II, C, 633 cites the following usage: "1616

Bullokar, *Colon*, 'A marke of a sentence not fully ended with is made with two prickes.'" All subsequent references in text as (*OED*).

2. James Agee and Walker Evans, *Let Us Now Praise Famous Men* ([1941] Boston: Houghton Mifflin, 1980), 44–45. All subsequent references are to this edition and are located parenthetically within the text.

3. *The Letters of James Agee to Father Flye* (New York: George Braziller, 1962), 105. Subsequent references in text as *Flye*. Rufus is the name of the boy in *A Death in the Family*.

4. Robert Fitzgerald, ed. *The Collected Poems of James Agee* (New York: Ballantine, 1970), 9. Further references appear in text as *Poems*.

5. According to a 1743 grammar "A *Colon* [:] is commonly put in the Middle of a Sentence; as *my Bowels are troubled, my Heart is turned within me: for I have grievously rebelled*." In G. Fox, *Instructions for right spelling, and plain directions for reading and writing true English. With several delightful things, very useful and necessary, both for young and old, to read and learn. Early American Imprints, Series I: Evans, 1639–1800*. no. 5186, 72.

6. Jacques Derrida, *Of Grammatology*. Trans Gayatri Chakravorty Spivak (Baltimore: Johns Hopkins University Press, 1976), 144–145.

7. 1751 Chambers *Cycl.* s.v. (*OED*)

8. Ruth Lechlitner, "Alabama Tenant Families," *New York Herald Tribune Books* August 24, 1941: 10.

9. Emma had had an affair with Evans in the early 1930s; see Belinda Rathbone, *Walker Evans, A Biography* (Boston: Houghton Mifflin, 1995), 101.

10. In "Sem;eroti;cs; Colono:zat:on: Exclamat!ons!" Jennifer DeVere Broday offers a tour de force performance in prose form of the sexuality encoded in the archaic residues of the semicolon and colon. Of course Agee, as ever, got there first. *Punctuation: Art, Politics, Play* (Durham, NC: Duke University Press, 2008), 134–155.

11. A rare usage of the term colon is "a husbandman." "1606 G. W[oodcocke] tr. *Hist. Iustine* Gg 5a, 'His father was a Colone or tenant to the famous Senat Aurelius.'" (*OED* 633).

12. H. Ramsey Fowler, *The Little, Brown Handbook* (Boston: Longham, 1980), 310. Maintaining distinctions between forms

of punctuation appears as important as maintaining distinctions between classes. "Separative punctuation is thus divided into two classes—end punctuation and interior punctuation. [ ... ] [T]he confusion of the two—the use of end punctuation where interior punctuation belongs or *vice versa*—is the worst possible blunder in punctuation." Edwin C. Woolley, *The Mechanics of Writing: A Compendium of Rules regarding Manuscript-Arrangement, Spelling, the Compounding of Words, Abbreviations, the Representation of Numbers, Syllabication, the Use of Capitals, the Use of Italics, Punctuation, and Paragraphing* (Boston: D. C. Heath, 1909), 118–19.

13. "1748 J. Mason *Elocut.* 24 'A Comma Stops the Voice while we may privately tell one, a Semi Colon two; a Colon three: and a Period four'" (*OED*).

14. James Agee, *A Death in the Family* ([1956] New York: Avon, 1959), 19.

15. As Alan Pryce-Jones in his "Preface" to James Agee describes somewhat sarcastically the young altar boy, Richard, *The Morning Watch* (New York: Ballantine, 1966), vii. This saga of the all-night church vigil before Easter Sunday held by residents of a Catholic boarding school, ends with Richard and two other boys killing a large snake, which dies when Richard finally smashes its head, leaving its body still twitching: "He looked coldly at his trembling hand: bloody at the knuckles and laced with slime, which seemed to itch and to burn as it dried, it still held the rock" (144–45). Fist-fucking around the colon.

16. Laurence Bergreen, *James Agee, A Life* (New York: E. P. Dutton, 1984), 343.

17. Quoted in Rathbone, *Walker Evans*, 159.

18. Zoe Trodd, "The Calling of Two Creatures: Depression-era Collaboration and a Theory of Camera and Pen," AC:Collaborative (Summer 2005) http://www.artcircles.org/id24.html. For more on this see Paula Rabinowitz, *They Must Be Represented: The Politics of Documentary* (London: Verso, 1994), ch. 2 and 3.

19. In his structuralist analysis of *Folk Housing in Middle Virginia*, Henry Glassie notes how "[i]n structuring its inhabitants in relation to other people, the house, through the predictability of its lower floor plan, was cohesive, but the path it dictated

from the road to the house's center functioned as a separator" (Knoxville: University of Tennessee Press, 1975), 122.

20. Glassie, "The square is a constant, tying the houses of different times into a single tradition" (120).

21. W. E. B. Du Bois, *The Souls of Black Folk* ([1903] New York: Dover, 1994), 85.

22. "Avoid misusing the colon," categorically states Fowler, *The Little, Brown Handbook*, 310. Information on colon use from Michael Erard, "Colons Descending: An Interim Assessment" *English Today* 48 (October 1996): 43–44, see his citation of J. T. Dillon's analysis studies of colon use in titles.

23. Woolley, *Mechanics of Writing*, 107.

24. Charles Swain Thomas, Will David Howe, and Zella O'Hair, *Composition and Rhetoric* (New York: Longmans, Green, 1908), 436.

25. Michael Gold, "Go Left, Young Writers!" New Masses (January 1929): 3. As Michael Denning notes, in *The Cultural Front: The Laboring of American Culture in the Twentieth Century* (London: Verso, 1996), 203, Gold's 1929 call had been preceded by a Whitmanesque (actually, in its use of dashes, a Dickinsonian) list of possible "worker-correspondents" who in the future might contribute to the radical magazine.

> Confessions—diaries—documents
> Letters form hoboes, peddlars, small town atheists,
>    unfrocked clergymen and schoolteachers—
> Revelations by rebel chambermaids and night club waiters—
> The sobs of driven stenographers—
> The poetry of steelworkers—
> The wrath of miners—the laughter of sailors—
> Strike stories, prison stories, work stories—
> Stories by Communist, I.W.W. and other revolutionary
>    workers.
>              Michael Gold, "Editorial," New Masses (July 1928): 3.

26. It was not until 1955 when Thomas Johnson's *Complete Poems of Emily Dickinson* appeared that Dickinson's use of "dashes as a musical device" became apparent because in his edition: "Punctuation and capitalization remain unaltered" (Boston: Little, Brown, n.d), x. There are several interpretations of Dickinson's jerky use of the dash that seek to make sense of them as musical or elocutionary notations, but for Kamilla Denman "Dickinson creates a haunting, subversive, impelling harmony

of language, wordless sound (emotional tonality and musical rhythms), and silence" (189). "Emily Dickinson's Volcanic Punctuation," in *Emily Dickinson: A Collection of Critical Essays*, ed. Judith Farr (Upper Saddle River, NJ: Prentice Hall, 1996), 187–205.

# 7

## ANIMATING THE GUDGERS: ON THE PROBLEMS OF A CINEMATIC AESTHETIC IN *LET US NOW PRAISE FAMOUS MEN*

### *Caroline Blinder*

The possibility that James Agee's writing interrogates the limitations and not just the advantages of the photographic image in *Let Us Now Praise Famous Men* has—perhaps understandably—been neglected in many previous readings.[1] For obvious reasons, Walker Evans's stature as a seminal photographer of the 1930s coupled with the innovatory nature of his collaboration with Agee in *Famous Men* has led to a focus on the interaction between image and text as predominantly photographic by nature. Nevertheless, as an entry into a wider understanding of Agee's literary aesthetic this chapter examines how the visual is configured in a wider sense in *Famous Men* and, in particular, how this illuminates Agee's desire to present the Gudger household in sacred terms. Written by a future film critic and a writer continuously revising and rethinking his ideas about the visual, the section on the Gudgers uses the maneuverability of a cinematic as well as a static photographic lens as a metaphor for how to animate, rather than merely capture, the lives of the sharecroppers. In this context, Agee's "animation" operates on two levels; in a cinematic sense it gives the appearance of movement and presence, in a spiritual and sacred sense it brings to life metaphorically and figuratively the existence of the Gudgers.

*Famous Men* preempts Agee's later fame as a movie critic but little has been written on how such things as the lyricism and importance of gestures, movement, pace, and editing, emerge in Agee's actual writing. This has always struck me as a strange omission, particularly considering how a cinematically inclined modernist discourse inflects most of Agee's other work. In this instance, the section entitled "The altar," part of "The Front Bedroom" section in "The Gudger House," provides an alternative slant to the idea of the photographic as intrinsic to *Famous Men* and the ways in which the visual both accentuates and demarcates the limitations of Agee's project.[2] In the altar section, the cinematic propensities of *Famous Men* emerge not only as a fundamental part of the narrative of the sharecroppers but also as part of the unfolding narrative of Agee's self-discovery. The altar section illuminates how *Famous Men* is a narrative of objects and people animated through the lens of Agee the writer, as well as that of Walker Evans the photographer. As seen in the painstakingly expository descriptions of objects, which in many ways function as "props" in the sharecroppers' homes, Agee's devotion to detail and the authority given to the description of inanimate objects is extended to himself as a sort of camera eye. What I am particularly interested in are the ways in which the detailed exposition of objects is always concurrent with an indication of their framing, or one could say, with the ways in which things are situated vis-à-vis each other as is true for both cinema and photography. Through framing and sequencing, Agee embarks on a particular form of journey through the Gudger house, a pilgrimage toward the inner sanctum and sacred hub of the sharecroppers' lives. Agee in turn infuses the "altar" section of the Gudger house with a religiosity both internal and external, as the external reality of the house becomes a cipher for a distinctly "Ageean" form of animation as well as self-discovery.

The use of the phrase animation is a deliberate one, in this respect, as the altar section although apparently about inanimate objects, is grounded in movement rather than stasis. In this section—also named the tabernacle by Agee—the desire to connect the sacred with the vernacular, the divine with the mundane, is done by animation—objects are animated, and similar to cinematic props, given the task of being instrumental to the lives surrounding them. As in silent film, with its necessary onus on gestures to convey narrative and the use of intermediary text/captions to set the scene, Agee seeks a pure form of visualization from which to instil an equally untainted vision of the Gudgers. It is therefore no coincidence that the beginning of Agee's solitary journey through the section entitled "The Gudger House," part of the Shelter chapter in Part Two: Some Findings and Comments, starts with a potentially cinematic moment when the family leaves the house and descends into the horizon:

> Slowly they diminished along the hill path, she, and her daughter, and her three sons, in leisured enfilade beneath the light. The mother first, her daughter next behind, her eldest son, her straggler, whimpering; their bare feet pressed out of the hot earth gentle explosions of gold. She carried her youngest child, his knees locked simian across her, his light hands at her neck, and his erected head, hooded with night, next hers, swivelled mildly upon the world's globe, a periscope. The dog, a convoy, plaited his wanderings round them through the briars. She wore the flowerlike beauty of the sunbonnet in which she is shamed to appear before us. At length, well up the hill, their talking shrank and became inaudible, and at that point will give safe warning on the hill of their return. Their slanted bodies slowly straightened, one by one, along the brim and turned into the east, a slow frieze and sank beneath the brim, in order of their heights, masts foundered in a horizon; the dog, each of the walking children, at length; at last, the guileless cobra gloatings of the baby, the mother's tall, flared head.
>
> They are gone. (*FM*, 134)

As the procession descends into the horizon, reminiscent of the Dovchenko films that Agee will later review, the perspective is of the minute movements, such as the child turning its head, the dust of their footprints, as well as the larger scenic potential of the landscape. Like little heroic soldiers walking off to battle the elements, the dog forms a convoy and a sentinel, there is some "safe warning" of their return. The mother here is both Madonna and warrior simultaneously, the family unit nearly primordial as the son clutches her in a "simian" fashion.

Notwithstanding these symbolic gestures, which one could argue figure in much of the photography coming out of the Farm Security Administration, it is the movement of the family out of the house, out of frame, and the concurrent loss of sound, which is distinctly cinematic. Contrary to what might be a furtive or even guilty sense of displacement on Agee's behalf, the removal of the family is in this instance what enables an understanding of their lives, their interconnectedness, and above all their heroic and sacred stature. And, indeed, it is no coincidence that the Shelter section, of which the Gudger House forms a constituent part, starts with the subtitle: "I will go unto the altar of God" (*FM*, 122). In other words, the movement of the family away from their home is not only the initial gesture that sets off the camera/narrator, but it also marks the beginning of Agee's "pilgrimage," a pilgrimage which will be documented by Evans's "silent" shots of the house and its unoccupied interiors.

Although the departure of the family is often seen as a necessary precursor for the subsequent fetishizing of their home and possessions a great deal more is taking place, the scene—in effect—is being set for a form of conversion. The fact that Agee brings up a previous incident when he was young, masturbating as he made his way through the rooms of an empty house, becomes curiously secondary as the ensuing description has Agee prostrating himself before the "altar." In this respect, Agee's body, rather than a site for pleasure, is given "over" to the existence of the sharecroppers and the house in turn becomes an object of religious contemplation:

> It is not entirely otherwise now, in this inhuman solitude, the nakedness of this body which sleeps here before me, this tabernacle upon whose desecration I so reverentially proceed: yet it differs somewhat: for there is here no open sexual desire, no restiveness, nor despair: but the quietly triumphant vigilance of the extended senses before an intricate task of surgery, a deep stealthfulness, not for shame of the people, but in fear and in honor of the house itself, a knowledge of being at work. (*FM*, 137)

Configured as both surgeon and preacher, there are intimations of an autopsy performed here, and yet the aim is to heal the scared existence of the sharecroppers rather than to bury them. Similarly the preacherly role invokes a vision of another task often performed in the presence of both death and life, namely the sacrament. "This body which sleeps here before me" is both Agee's, the sharecropper's and Christ's, the ritual that Agee is engaged in one of confession as well as absolution. The fact that such rituals are centered in solitude as opposed to communal activity is another strange thing about *Famous Men*. For a book that seeks to salvage a dispossessed and disenfranchised group of people, they are manifestly not present for large stretches of time. When they are present the gestures and signs that they convey are infinitely more important than any articulated discourse. The language at play here is, rather, a language based on Agee's ability to decipher those details—the mother's slow turning of the head, the placement of things on the mantelpiece—that are symptomatic of the Gudgers' lives.

This "silent language" of the sharecroppers sits both comfortably and uncomfortably in the space between cinema and photography, a space—one could argue—where a precarious balance is struck between stillness and movement, between life and death in the Gudger home. For Agee, this is also the space where the interior life of the Gudger family is aligned with that of his own. Rather than question the primacy of the visible world, Agee seeks in a metaphysical sense to align the interior space of humanity with its outer parameters, or—one could say—make the house speak for the family. As John Dorst argues, the threshold that constitutes the opening between exterior and interior space in the Gudger house is also meta-phorically the space that Agee the intruder/narrator/interme-diary occupies, in ways similar to that of the camera eye.

If that threshold is metaphorically aligned with the camera lens it is, for Dorst, a partially alienating device; a device that pro-vides a false sense of safety and a screen of sorts. Although this clearly has repercussions for the ethnographic and social aspects of the project, in aesthetic terms it presents us with an image of Agee "screened off" and hindered from emulating Evans's photographic mastery. The fact that Agee constantly compares his own defects as a writer against Evans's abilities in mimetic, documentary, as well as ethical terms, does not however mean that he wants to be Evans. In fact, as Agee constantly battles with the definition of what actually constitutes a documentary ethos, his disqualifying comments regarding his own abilities have to be taken with a large grain of salt. If Agee's protests are performative when it comes to the issue of writing vis-à-vis photography, they also sharpen and question the very nature of what constitutes realism and what its place should be within a documentary ethos. The fact that Agee speaks of photography as containing aesthetic possibilities, which writing can only seek to imitate, does not mean in other words, that he necessarily wants to be engaged in "photographic writing." More accu-rately Agee seeks to excavate through visual means the inner life of his subjects. One such example is what Agee unearths in the Gudger's tabernacle, here the most prosaic of sacred objects, a torn up old newspaper article, becomes significant:

(To the left:)
    NEW STRIKE MOVE
    EARED AS PEACE

NFAB SPLITS UP

‑

fer to Arbitrate is
Down by Real
e Group

—

s Owners
f Parley
Labour
Reat

The writing stems from a torn up newspaper article but here it reads more like a coded message, its captions/titles reminiscent of newsreel footage and wry commentaries on the archaeological nature of Agee's investigation. Like ancient hieroglyphs the ragged newsprint is deliberately presented to us "raw," without intermediary explanation.

Like so many other instances in *Famous Men*, the captions are charged precisely because they say a great deal without any discursive context. This does not detract from the political subtext. The larger political and economic problems may be left unspoken but they nevertheless affect the minutiae of the Gudgers' house. For Agee the context is quite literally there, he is standing in the midst of it: the house of the Gudgers, the circumstances of their lives. Hence the words strike, arbitration, owners, labor, signal not only the inevitable encroachment of the outside world but also the fact that this outside world, despite having such huge economic ramifications, comes through only as curiously incomplete. In the face of the sharecropper's reality, newspaper print can be no more than arbitrary and ineffective signage. If signage for Evans is revelatory and beautiful in a photographic sense, the paper print for Agee, although charged with an otherworldliness both mystical and real, can only speak to us through a broken code. It signals—perhaps—that the Gudgers are aware that they are part of a larger more pervasive problem. Not unlike the translucent denim material of the sharecropper's overhauls, which Agee later describes, the humanity of the sharecroppers is likewise imprinted into the very fabric of the text. Like the worn material of their clothing, the old newspaper clippings are nearly translucent even if their meanings are not. Like a negative, Agee insinuates, "held against the light, the contents of both sides of the paper are visible at once" (*FM*, 169).

**Figure 7.1**   Walker Evans, "Fireplace and Wall Detail" 1936

*Source*: Courtesy of Library of Congress, Prints and Photographs Division, FSA-OWI Collection [Reproduction number: LC-USF342-008135-A].

If the written word, in this instance, shares the translucent property of so many objects it is a translucency, which is near impossible to capture. This is partly why Evans's photograph of the "tabernacle" seems akin to a still life, the objects we see are placed strategically, they are solid if damaged, and they speak of a certain gravitas and melancholy. Agee, on the other hand, takes a different approach and animates what appears to be entirely inanimate. Given the task of aligning the poet's lyrical eye with the ability to bring things to life Agee adopts the perspective not of a still, but of a moving camera:

> here a moving camera might know, on its bareness, the stand-
> ing of the four iron feet of a bed, the wood of a chair, the
> scrolled treadle of a sewing machine, the standing up at right
> angles of plain wood out of plain wood, the great and hand-
> some grains and scars of this vertical and prostrate wood, the
> huge and noble motions of brooms and of knees and of feet,
> and how with clay, and animals, and the leaning face of a
> woman, these are among the earliest and profoundest absorp-
> tions of a very young child. (*FM*, 149)

The poet's voice shares the characteristics of the cinematic eye, albeit one that adopts a childlike perspective, lying on the floor looking upward and toward the movement of adult-hood. In this sense, the cinematic perspective is recuperative, remembering, and simultaneously creative and ongoing. As in Hebrew mythology, the presence of clay intimates a terri-tory in which animation has sacred proportions, the implica-tion being that all creatures, human and animal are made here.

The childlike image of Agee prostrate on the floor is of course another way to engage with the Gudgers in a nonvoy-euristic fashion. Agee's awareness that he is trespassing on holy ground is thus facilitated by his adopted perspective, a perspective which sets us up for the encounter with the altar:

> And, centred one upon another and at centre of their square-
> spread partition wall, all squarely opposite the square window,

the table and the fireplace and the mantel which, with the wall, create a shrine and altar. (*FM*, 162)

The positioning and description of the altar accentuates its centrality in terms of its location within the household as well as within the text. In this respect, the Gudgers' house is not just described as a church or churchlike environment, it is a church. The proof of divine design lies in the neat symmetry of the location of the altar and the secular nature of what constitutes it: the table, the fireplace, and the mantel. These things "squarely" and honestly are meant to remind us of a past life and the proof of this life lies in the remnants of objects kept for posterity, signs of things lost and loved.

On the table: it is blue auto paint: a white cloth, hanging a little over the edges. On the cloth, at centre, a small fluted green glass bowl in which sits a white china swan, profiled upon the north. (*FM*, 163)

Blues and greens and the translucency of glass are all things that cannot be captured by Evans's austere black and white, but more importantly, they speak once again of the importance of location and how things are placed within it. The white china swan is profiled upon the north, the bowl is carefully centered all, in other words, is in its exact place. This accentuates the altar as a location with significance and an appropriate site for the attempted retrieval of a rapidly vanishing past, a past that is particular and photographic. On the mantel that forms part of the altar is "A fading box-camera snapshot: low, grey, dead-looking land stretched back in a deep horizon; twenty yards back, one corner of the tenant house, central at the foreground, two women" (*FM*, 163).

The fading box camera snapshot, although seemingly outmoded and out of date like the newspaper clipping, is a stark reminder of the sense of loss and displacement that permeates the landscape. Just as Evans's photographs, this image shares a sense of the static and meditative nature of the location.

The women may be "central at the foreground," but their anonymity renders them strangely without agency, as though they too are waiting to be animated by some external force. As such, they and the objects beside them form a necessary precursor for Agee's ability to animate them, to give their vernacular status a sense of actual spiritual life. The objects are what they are, not merely because they have been invested with so much Benjaminian aura, but because they are vessels for all the failed aspirations and desires of their owners. Because they have no inherent qualities and no information that overtly disturbs their talismanic value Agee can proffer them up as veritable relics and proof of the sharecroppers' survival. From an economic standpoint these objects point to the fact that their owners once had bourgeois aspirations; in a spiritual sense, they prove the possibility of regeneration, of the sharecroppers' uncanny ability, like Christ, to rise again.

In the tabernacle itself Agee painstakingly describes the worn baptismal clothes of the Gudger children as though he wants to restitch them himself. The tactile nature of his description and general wonderment at the quotidian makes it tempting to see Agee's fetishization of objects as similar to the Surrealist's fascination with the found object. Breton's "the quotidian marvellous," the lifting of any object that an artist may "stumble on during a walk...to the rank of the work of art," also lends itself to a reading of the everyday as infused with both aesthetic and political possibilities.[3] Despite this, Agee's religiosity, which is made manifest in the Gudger house, makes it something fundamentally different.[4]

For the Surrealists, found objects are charged with the marvellous because they speak to us on a nonverbal level of subconscious desires, fears, and longings, allowing—in other words—an intermediary space for the free play of the unconscious. Like Agee, Breton was enamored by the idea that everyday objects could become props, as it were, for a poetic engagement with the surrounding world. In Agee's case, the objects on the altar clearly allow such an engagement, but they are less so proof of the perseverance of the unconscious.

Looking more closely at the objects partly illuminates this; to accentuate the desire-driven aspect of found objects the Surrealists favored objects with no discernible use and/or a rapidly obsolete use value, hence the fascination with scrap, junkyards, flea markets, and so on.[5]

For Agee, on the other hand, the objects found must in some way be necessary and part of a living functional economy, utilized daily by those to whom they belong even if they are kept in place as a memorial to something, which they cannot have. It is the fact that obsolete tools are continuously used, that random knives and forks constitute a complete set of utensils, that the smell of yesterday's sweat is still ingrained in the fabric and material, which enables Agee to reanimate them in a lyrical sense.[6]

The Tabernacle
In the table drawer, in this order:
A delicate insect odour of pine, closed sweated cloth, and mildew.
One swooning-long festal baby's dress of the most frail muslin, embroidered with three bands of small white cotton-thread flowers. Two narrow courses of cheap yet small-threaded lace are let in near the edge of the shirt. This garment is hand-sewn in painfully small and laboured stitchings. It is folded, but not pressed, and is not quite clean. (*FM*, 165)

Like a shroud the material and indeed materiality at hand here is made all the more human by taking on the qualities of those who have made them. Or to put it differently, things are sacred because even in their ability to decay they become living proof of humanity's proximity to God. The issue is not merely that the clothing described predates a commercial sensibility or that it is hand-sewn and not store-bought, what is crucial is that it is labored in an act of love. *Famous Men*—as Agee reiterates—is about the "predicaments of human divinity" and if so, the predicament, the schism between the sacred and the all too blatantly secular lives of these sharecroppers is evident in what they have and what they do not have. The lace on the baby's dress may be cheap but the workmanship involved is extraordinary.

This blurring of objectification attests to Agee's anxieties about what to do with the things he finds and yet it remains a crucial element in his fascination with the capturing of both human movement and stasis, with life and death. The altar provides Agee with the opportunity to represent the share-croppers as both spiritual and actual human beings, as living beings animated by Agee "in the now" as well as captured for posterity through the iconicity of Evans's photographs. To complicate matters further, it is hard to decipher whether Agee uses the camera lens as a metaphor for the intermediary position of the poet's visionary eye, or the camera body as a metaphor for the artist in the process of recording. While Agee does not want to defend one position over another his desire to reenact and capture the spirituality of the sharecrop-pers necessitates a lens flexible enough to capture a sense of permanence as well as flux.

This conundrum manifests itself in work predating *Famous Men* as well. In "notes for a moving picture: the house" Agee positions himself as a moving, roaming, and intrinsically self-reflexive camera:

> the camera settles gently to rest in the dark front hallway before an ornate hatrack and looks at itself close and hard in the mirror, beginning very softly to purr (the reduced dry sound of its motor); swings back to centre of hall, beneath centre of stairwell, and delicately takes flight, swinging slowly round so that with not perfect regularity the upward swing and bulge of the banister swings with its eye."[7]

Comparable with the more famous moment in the Gudger house where

> the silence of the brightness of this middle morning is increased upon me moment by moment and upon this house,

and upon this house the whole of heaven is drawn into one
lens; and this house itself, in each of its objects, it, too, is one
lens. (*FM*, 136)

In "Notes for a moving picture," the film concerns itself less
with a house and more with the narrator as a sort of motion
controlled camera. The operative image is that of Agee as
the eye/lens looking at itself "close and hard in the mirror," a purring machine whose delicate flight up the banister
seeks to embody the essence of a location in flux, animated
through movement. Agee's use of the camera as a metaphor
for the artist's eye in this aborted piece of cinematic writing
begins a complex confluence of time and photography, not
dissimilar to Agee's later view of the sharecroppers' home. In
a decidedly Emersonian moment, the lens becomes, like the
transparent eyeball, an intermediary for whom the activity of
focusing is akin to the lyrical gesture of writing as a form of
self-fashioning, of creating the world one inhabits. No wonder then that the house itself, in each of its objects, it, too,
is one lens.

Couched in this Emersonian moment of the purely epiphanous, Agee exposes himself (not unlike Thoreau) to the
elements

> beneath upward coilings of transparent air, and here, their
> home; and they have gone; and it is now my chance to perceive
> this, their home, as it is, in whose hollow heart resounds the
> loud zinc flickering heartbeat of the cheap alarm two hours
> advanced upon false time; a human shelter, a strangely lined
> nest, a creature of killed pine, stitched together with nails into
> about as rude a garment against the hostilities of heaven as
> human family may wear. (*FM*, 137)

Through the epiphanous, perspective merges with a sense of
the house as holy ground. As the inhabitants are "gone" their
surroundings become vital extensions, clothes, armatures, ves-
tal garments for the sharecroppers to embody figuratively and

metaphorically. In the same way, the house becomes a "nest" lined with relics that Agee cannot help but handle, a church full of sacred objects.[8] The fact that this epiphanous quality is made visible in Agee's ability to conjure up movement, to provide an animated sense of otherwise static objects, does not prove its superiority to the static camera lens, nor would it be wise to see a direct reversal of Evans's static gaze in Agee's roaming eye. After all, cinema's ability to portray movement is always an extension of the still image—one follows the other—as is essentially the definition of film. Agee needs Evans's meditative camera. In fact, he reminds us of this incessantly, the sense of time being stopped and classified to allow for the shock of movement. Agee's preoccupation with animation is thus also with the animation of things and places that would otherwise be lifeless.

The return to the altar partly proves this. In both Agee's description and the photograph by Evans of the altar, the background/wall behind the altar/tabernacle carries "at the right of the mantel, in whitewash, all its whorlings sharp, the print of a child's hand" (*FM*, 165). The print of a child's hand immediately adjacent to the tabernacle, the receptacle of the sacrament, could not be a more apt image of the actual imprint of humanity within a sacred sphere just as it is an imprint of time past. The handprint instills on the viewer a sense of the importance of—literally and figuratively—the human touch, just as it mimics the art of cave dwellings, the nature of testimonials, fingerprints, talismanic signs, and religious signage.

The child's hand print accentuates Agee's role as he who deciphers the traces of lives lived, and by extension, proves the camera's ability to move beyond the surface of things rather than merely intimate their existence. In a poetic sense it is as though Agee tentatively reaches out for something that he has yet to articulate, namely the hand of the child as well as the imprint of the artist absolved of all sins and presumptions. Agee, with his Jesuit background, would have been familiar with the tabernacle as the most holy of repositories and the original sanctuary for the Ark of the Covenant during the

Israelite exodus. In more ways than one, the tabernacle is a fitting expression for the displacement of the sharecroppers as a Diaspora community economically and socially adrift in America.[9]

Of all the many votive offerings in *Famous Men*—the book in a sense one as well—the prime purpose of the altar section is to render the visible through the invisible. The fact that the altar is of no apparent value, that the mantelpiece is like all others in the region, is what makes it stand out as a genuine altar. The room is a church because this mantel is an altar, and it is an altar because it contains offerings that are revelatory.

The revelatory nature of the cinematic was ultimately confirmed for Agee in the 1940s, but to me, it appears as something he suspected much earlier, namely that there is always something beyond the frame, something, which the still camera can only intimate. Not coincidentally, the torn newspaper in the altar section also contains a description of two night scenes from undisclosed films:

1. A man in civilian clothes, including gloves, back to, is doing something unidentifiable to what may be an elevator door.
2. A Street. Two policemen. One is balanced in recoil from an action just accomplished. The face signifies un-huh. The other, glasses, a masterful head, his nightstick just rebounding from the palm-clenched skull of a hatless topcoated civilian whose head is level with his hips" (*FM*, 167).

From the careful lyricism of the objects on the altar, the fluted glass, the frail muslin in the tabernacle, Agee suddenly shifts to something much more prosaic. In these stills, possibly from news footage of fights between police and strike sympathizers, the images are not only the antithesis to Evans's measured interiors but also stark reminders of photography's inability to tell the full story. Just as the incomplete captions and newspaper headings, it is what we cannot see, the "something unidentifiable," "the recoil from an action just accomplished," which tells us something important may have happened. Despite the political context, the setups in these photographs are what tell the story and the details, if any, must come later. Agee must have known that his deliberate use of such discordant material would both accentuate the beauty of the sharecroppers' home and complicate his deification of them.

Agee's insistence that the poet sees *through* his eyes rather than with them, that the act of looking is always about being an intermediary is what is at stake here and what inevitably complicates the idea of a static as well as moving lens. Like so many vernacular modernists of the 1930s Agee makes the poet's visionary abilities "camera like" in order to stress the meditative aspect of the process rather than its strict recording ability. It is this which muddles the ethnographic process and both taints and elevates the documentary work. It is this, also, which enables Agee to align the cinematic eye with the eye of the poet seeking redemption. Here is a project, which aims for no less than to prove the redemptive power of sight, even as it hinges on enabling that which is nearly impossible, namely the writing out of a composite and distinctly visual epiphany. If Agee's vision works by a curious prolepsis of the secular and the sacred its aim is to prove the sacredness of the families investigated. The problem, of course, is that such a vision, like the very existence of the Gudger family, relies on an accumulative, messy, and potentially neverending process of documentation.[10]

What Agee is so wonderfully inept at and what he perseveres with nonetheless is a kind of poetic archaeology that works through and despite the constant swerving between still and moving image. What makes his task impenetrable is the acknowledgment that the epiphanous moment, while desirable, is also impossible. There can be no atemporal Emersonian vision in the Gudger house, no single object on the altar can tell the full story; no careful delineation of architectural circumstance can accurately measure the parameters of the existence under scrutiny. Without any subterfuge Agee insists on aligning the interior archaeology of his mind and the exterior archaeology of the unearthing—almost literally—of the constituent parts of the Gudger family. In the end, what we see externally is what attaches value to interior life and for Agee "the writing on the wall" like the child's hand at the "tabernacle" provides the direct link to the epiphanous and the illuminatory. Perhaps the Gudgers carry an emphatic charge not because Evans's images have memorialized them so well, but because through Agee's ability to animate them, they were once unmistakably alive.

## NOTES

1. James Agee and Walker Evans, *Let Us Now Praise Famous Men* ([1941] Boston: Houghton Mifflin, 1988). All subsequent references are to this edition and are located within the text.
2. Which in turn is in the Shelter Section of Part Two: Some Findings and Comments in Book Two.
3. André Breton, *What Is Surrealism: Selected Writings* (London: Pluto Press, 1978), 352.
4. See also Hugh Davis, "The Making of James Agee" Doctoral Dissertation (Knoxville: University of Tennessee, 2005). Through a comparative analysis of Surrealist ideology and aesthetics vis-à-vis the work of Agee, Davis makes a strong case for not underestimating the continental influence on Agee's work.
5. To some extent, the Gudger family overall could be read as an "objet trouvé," the implication being that Agee's romance with them and their situation is highly marked by their imminent demise in political and economic terms. This carries a disturbing set of connotations, which deserve some consideration.
6. This argument, I realise, is easily complicated by the Surrealists' fascination with, for example, Eugene Atget's images of shop fronts, a fascination shared by many documentary photographers. The lineages at work here are complex. We know that Berenice Abbot showed her Atget prints to Walker Evans, and we know that Evans's later work is clearly relatable to Atget and Surrealism as well.
7. James Agee, *The Collected Short Prose* (London: Calder and Boyars, 1972), 166.
8. Kazin is right to point to the similarity between Agee and Faulkner (see also Mick Gidley's chapter). The false time of the cheap

alarm clock in this section brings to mind the issue of Time in Faulkner's *The Sound and the Fury*, which Agee would certainly have read.

9. Coincidences abound in the religiosity of so much Depression era documentary work (after all Dorothea Lange's version from 1939 was aptly named American Exodus), but here, it is also in a different sense about a more private religiosity and about Agee's attempt to revive his own faith.

10. Yves de Laurot in "From Logos to Lens" (1970) speaks of a proleptic vision:

"The filmmaker makes metaphor because he has to, out of an inner necessity: there is no other way to project his moral vision upon the reality his consciousness has shown him to exist. In other words, revolutionary metaphor is the result of the conscience acting on the knowledge the consciousness provides. The important point to make here is that this vision has to exist before creation: in fact, were it not for this vision, there would be no reaction, no true creation in the revolutionary sense. Because a work of art is the man's projection beyond the real—it is the inevitable praxis that stems from his moral needs." Yves de Laurot, "From Logos to Lens" in *Movies and Methods* Vol. 1, ed. Bill Nichols (Berkeley: University of California Press, 1976), 582.

# Epilogue

# Agee and Evans:
# "On The Porch: 4"

*William Stott*

We do not know as much as we would like to know about Agee and Evans's collaboration on *Let Us Now Praise Famous Men,* but we do have a few facts on good authority.

FACT ONE: we know that Agee and Evans talked about what they were doing. We know this because Agee tells us so in the last paragraph of the book. Late at night, he and Evans are on the Gudgers's porch, one of them lying on a car seat, when they hear what they take to be the warbling of foxes. After this, Agee writes,

> we began a little to talk. Ordinarily we enjoyed talking and of late, each absorbed throughout most of the day in subtle and painful work that made even the lightest betrayal of our full reactions unwise, we had found the fragments of time we were alone, and able to give voice to them and to compare and analyze them, valuable and necessary beyond comparison of cocaine.[1]

They talked, but what did they say? We would love to know. Agee's script for the unproduced movie "Noa-Noa" (1953) imagines conversations between Paul Gauguin and Vincent van Gogh. And are they embarrassing!

> VINCENT Do you want to know the real trouble with you?
> GAUGUIN As a matter of fact: yes.
> VINCENT For all your bragging about being "primitive,"
> you're afraid of everything really primitive.
> GAUGUIN Am I?
> VINCENT Yes, you are. You're afraid of Nature, and afraid of
> your emotions.[2]

Or:

> GAUGUIN Do you know, Vincent? I want to paint your por-
> trait.
> VINCENT Really?
> GAUGUIN NODS.
> VINCENT Well. Well. I'm—very much flattered. But we'll
> have to wait till I finish my sunflowers; I'm sorry but—
> GAUGUIN Go right ahead with them. That's how I want to
> paint you.[3]

The Gauguin–van Gogh conversations are generally better than this suggests. But they are embarrassing because we
know these are Great Men Talking, and what they say cannot
match their greatness and best not try to.

More than a decade ago, associates of Robert Redford's
Sundance Institute bought the rights to make a commercial
movie of *Famous Men,* which would focus on Agee and Evans.
I cringe at the dialogue I imagine: "Walker, I tell you these
are my people. This is where I belong." "Now, Jim, you gotta
be careful. These are simple folk, and it's too easy to make
them fall in love with you." "Walker, everybody has got to do
what he feels in this world, or else he dies." "Jimmy, I tell you
these women aren't going to understand if you start moving
up on them." "Walker, I was thinking of you...and me...and
them."

FACT TWO: if we believe Evans, no dialogue remotely
like the last took place. Asked about Agee's suggestion that he
and Evans and Annie-Mae and George Gudger and Emma,
Annie-Mae's sister, all thought about having group sex, Evans

told my wife and me in 1971, "I blush and squirm every time I read that. God! In the first place, it wasn't in my mind at all. Agee never mentioned it. But my God, the enormity of such a suggestion." My guess is that Agee and Evans' bedtime talk about their work consisted of grunts of satisfaction:

> Going O.K?
> Yeah. Wonderful stuff.
> —requests for elbow room—
> I'd like to shoot the kitchen tomorrow.
> O.K., I'll work the bedroom.
> —and calls to attention—
> Did you see the dress she had on?
> George loves that mechanic's cap.
> —which, I suspect, were quickly acknowledged and silenced—
> Um-un.
> Yeah, I saw that.

Even such minimal talk is an embarrassment. What Agee and Evans said will never be known and, as far as I am concerned, cannot be plausibly recreated. Despite Agee's putting their conversation "above cocaine," maybe there was not much of it. "Our days were very full and busy," Walker told us in 1971. "We hardly had time to speak to each other. He [Agee] was out working and I was out working. We agreed to go our separate ways."

FACT THREE: We know, or at least I hope to convince you, that Agee looked up to Evans and sought Evans's encouragement and help in writing the book. Evans was of course six years older than Agee—a substantial number of years when you are twenty-six, as Agee was in the summer of 1936. Evans was the more established artist. Evans had a job, photographing rural life pretty much as he chose to for the U.S. government, which Agee certainly considered much better than his assigned writing for *Fortune* magazine.

Furthermore, Agee had a way of looking up—and I must add, cozying up; disciple-ing himself—to anybody for whom he had respect. He shows himself doing this with his famous people, the Gudgers and Bud Woods and Frank and Sadie Ricketts, and he did it with Evans. In still-unpublished letters to Evans written while he was working on *Famous Men,* Agee solicits not only Evans's pity for the hardness of the task he, Agee, has set himself but also Evans's counsel on how he can do it better. Pity first. Here's from a letter of June 30, 1938:

I've been in a long, blind streak on the work: less inactive than non-resultant and circular; eight or ten drafts of a thing probably not even to be used.[4]

August 24, 1938:

I hardly know what to say of my work, except that I still have the feeling of doing it all wrong.[5]

Now a long paragraph from July 1, 1938:

I feel rather well though not over the working the last two or three days, which has been pretty hard and bulky—but I realize that actually I hardly know the meaning, much less the method, of one really hard and full day's work after another over a long period: and besides ignorance and lack of discipline, there are lots of unconscious tricks and blockades, exhausting and sickening me, paralyzing the word-mechanism in proportion to the seriousness and verticality of the would-be attack, and in general more frustrating and diluting me than I can get at to rectify. All I can do at present is to violently and strictly attack every deterrent within conscious reach: and even that is for some again sinister reason made to seem harder and more painful to do than I can describe. Several times a day it becomes physically impossible to sit and write even through another sentence: and having stood up and walked around it is hard to get back into as (for me) stepping into a cold bath is-add, if the cold bath were also hot oil. The only way to do it seems to be simplemindedly or mindlessly—which is the only way I can manage the cold bath: but it is very annoying and disturbing to me that I shouldn't manage to be fully and mentally eager to take hold of the work. Something is damn seriously wrong that I'm not: probably that I'm mistaken in thinking that I should try to write or Art at all, I don't know. I expect I had sooner or later better find out, though.[6]

Now pleas for direct help. Agee to Evans in an undated letter of December 1938:

> I'm trying to write about Mrs. Burroughs [Mrs. Gudger, as she is called in the book]. I wonder whether you have or could without too much trouble get what you once wrote about her, and whether you'd be willing that I use it intact as just what it is, afterward commenting or not as seemed best. I would want to extremely if you feel agreeable to the idea yourself.[7]

Evans wrote about the sharecroppers? Where? Why? What did he say? We are unlikely ever to know.

According to Evans, when Harper and Brothers turned down *Famous Men,* Agee asked him to edit the manuscript to make it more palatable for other publishers. Evans refused to take their collaboration to this level. "I said, 'Absolutely not. I won't. I won't touch it,'" he said in 1971. "Although I saw—I could have edited it—I saw things that needed to be done. But I thought that it was too great and that its faults had better be left in it. Even though it needed it, it wasn't I who was going to touch it."

In fact, however, the closest thing we have to the original manuscript—a second carbon copy of a late, typed draft at the University of Texas at Austin—shows that in at least one instance Evans contributed to the book's revision. Agee had written that the tenant farmer called Bud Woods was visited by "a man dressed as a city man might dress whose work was in the country, an organizer, say." Evans commented in the margin: "This might get Fields [i.e., Bud Woods] in trouble and is doubtful anyway. Why not remove it?" Agee cut the passage from the published text.[8] The last piece of evidence about Agee's veneration of Evans is the most curious. Agee felt much closer to the sharecropper families than Evans did.

In later years, Agee wrote to them, once visited, and sent presents. Evans's comparative indifference to the sharecroppers ("I'd said all I wanted to about them," he said in 1971) made Agee ashamed of his own feelings. On December 21, 1938, Agee sent Evans this apologetic postcard:

> Walker—I broke down and sent or am sending various things to the Tingles Fields & Burroughs; took liberty of saying they are "from" you as well; hope that's o.k.; am letting you know in case you need [illegible] any modification if possible write to them. Would again suggest (but I know you are damned busy & I apologize) that the pictures you told them you'd send would mean a lot to the Tingles. Love, J.[9]

Because, I would argue, Agee so needed to feel himself mentored, approved of by an older man he respected (we remember his father died when he was six), he very much wanted to see the book as a collaboration, and many times refers to it as such. He tried to give Evans half the royalties, and Evans had to insist to get only one-quarter, a generous percentage given the time the book required of him compared with Agee. Evans, if we take him at his word, considered *Famous Men* primarily Agee's book. In 1974 he wrote, "I feel that I have come into too much prominence on the tail of Agee's genius. I regard *Let Us Now Praise Famous Men* as his book—and it certainly is."[10]

This leads me to a final point about Agee and Evans' collaboration. It was Agee's book, but Agee could only do it with *Evans*—an Evans. For, if we are symbolists or lovers of archetype, are not Agee and Evans two components of every piece of documentary reporting? Don't all successful documentary practitioners have an Agee and an Evans in them?

Agee loves fieldwork but has great difficulty reducing it into a final form. So much does he love the process of gathering that he extends it interminably in his mind, repeats the contact experience over and over till his imagination has made pretty much everything possible of it. Driving to New York to deliver

the manuscript more than a year late to Harpers, Agee realized as he neared the George Washington Bridge that there
was another way the book could be organized, and turned
around and drove back to Frenchtown, New Jersey, to redo
it. A putter-inner, Agee cannot stop adding, tacking footnotes
to footnotes in the final galleys, never wanting to let go of
his firsthand and vicarious (through memory and imagination and art) experience of the wondrous world he has found
and recreated. Agee is, in a word, an amateur; he is playing
the game for love. He sees documentary work as an endless
romance with the other.

Evans, on the other hand, is a pro. He sees the assignment
as a job. He covers his ass and all bases. *Fortune* brought him
in especially for the work and he means to please. There is
a possibility *Fortune* will want to run a *Life* magazine style
"photo essay" on sharecropping (though *Life* won't be on the
newsstands for another six months, and it will be nine months
before Henry Luce coins the phrase "photo essay," the concept is already well known), so Evans takes photos (most still
unpublished, but look at the FSA file) that imply aspects of
sharecropping—planting, for example—that did not happen
during his weeks in Alabama.

Whereas Agee loses himself in whatever he undertakes,
Evans says he always asked himself: "What can I spend of
myself on this...merde?" After a two weeks shooting in the
field, Evans thinks maybe he has enough, and he has Agee
drive him to Birmingham so he can get clean and develop
his negatives in the hotel sink or bathtub and see where the
project stands. Agee drops Evans in Birmingham and turns
around and heads back to the field, fearing he will miss out on
something crucial (in fact the torrential night of his return he
happens into what he will learn later, through his writing of
it, is the center of his quest: Annie-Mae and George Gudgers's
acceptance of him as a long-lost part of their family).

Harpers gives Evans half as many pages as he wants for
pictures: so Evans does the job in two signatures instead of
four (a pro is always a taker-outer). When Houghton-Mifflin

wants to reprint the book in 1960, Evans insists on four signatures, sixty-four pages, and, adding, dropping, and recropping pictures, makes the book's photo section into (he admits) "another composition," although he had not intended to. He does this without going through his chaotic files to see if he put aside better images than those he used in the first edition and gave the FSA. (As indeed he had: the picture of the Gudgers and Emma on Sunday, which he came across and first printed for his 1971 MOMA retrospective). A pro knows when something's good enough and does not try to gild a lily.

I suggest that, symbolically, Agee's is the passion that turns a boilerplate assignment into an act of love. Evans's is the cold-blooded commonsense—Evans liked to call himself "a classicist," after all—that gets the job on track and finished. Agee and Evans had traveled through the South for nearly a month, the full time of their assignment, before they found their subjects. It was not Agee who found the sharecroppers—though, as we have seen, he would care about them much more and in a different way from Evans. No, Agee, the romantic butterfly at this stage of his life was too entranced by the process of looking and the riches of possibility to stick to one place or person; and he was too shy to make a nuisance of himself. Evans, the pragmatist, knew there was an assignment to save, so he sauntered up to the men later known as Bud Woods, Fred Ricketts, and George Gudger in the town square that Saturday and started chatting with them about the weather, we suppose, and the price of crops, and put in motion the project that makes them all immortal.

## NOTES

1. James Agee and Walker Evans, *Let Us Now Praise Famous Men* (Boston: Houghton Mifflin, 1960), 140.
2. James Agee, *Agee on Film* (New York: McDowell and Obolensky, 1958), 2 Vols.
3. Ibid.
4. Unpublished letter from James Agee to Walker Evans; quoted with permission from the James Agee Papers at the Harry Ransom

Humanities Research Center at the University of Texas at Austin. The author wishes to thank the wonderful HRC staff and friends he has worked with over the years: Joe Colthrop, David Farmer, Roy Flukinger, Cathy Henderson, Sally Leach, Mae MacNamara, John Payne, and Sheree Scarborough.

5. Ibid.
6. Ibid.
7. Ibid.
8. Ibid.
9. Ibid.
10. In "Walker Evans: Photographs from the 'Let Us Now Praise Famous Men' Project" (booklet), ed. William Stott and David Farmer, Humanities Research Center, University of Texas at Austin, 1974.

# SELECTED BIBLIOGRAPHY

Agee, James, *The Collected Poems of James Agee*, edited and with an introduction by Robert Fitzgerald (London: Calder and Boyars, 1972).

———, *The Collected Short Prose of James Agee*, edited by Robert Fitzgerald (London: Calder and Boyars, 1972).

———, *A Death in the Family* ([1956] New York: Avon, 1959).

———, *Letters of James Agee to Father Flye* (New York: Braziller, 1962).

Agee, James, and Walker Evans, *Let Us Now Praise Famous Men* ([1941] Boston: Houghton Mifflin, 1960).

Augsburger, Michael, *An Economy of Abundant Beauty: Fortune Magazine and Depression America* (Ithaca, NY: Cornell University Press, 2004).

Bachelard, Gaston. *The Poetics of Space* (New York: Orion Press, 1964).

Barnouw, Dagmar. *Critical Realism: History, Photography, and the Work of Siegfried Kracauer* (Baltimore: Johns Hopkins University Press, 1994).

Barthes, Roland, *Camera Lucida* (New York: Noonday Press, 1981).

Bergreen, Laurence, *James Agee, A Life* (New York: E. P. Dutton, 1984).

Breton, André, *What Is Surrealism: Selected Writings* (London: Pluto Press, 1978).

Brown, Norman O., *Life against Death: The Psychoanalytical Meaning of History* (Middleton: Wesleyan University Press, 1972).

Carlton, David L., and Peter A. Coclanis, editors, *Confronting Southern Poverty in the Great Depression: The Report on Economic Conditions of the South with Related Documents* (New York: St. Martin's Press, 1996).

# 176    Selected Bibliography

Chase, Stuart, *The Tyranny of Words* (New York: Harcourt, Brace, 1938).

Clifford, James, and George E. Marcus, *Writing Culture: The Poetics and Politics of Ethnography* (Berkeley: University of California Press, 1986).

Coles, Robert, *Doing Documentary Work* (New York: Oxford University Press, 1997).

Crary, Jonathan, *Techniques of the Observer: On Vision and Modernity in the Nineteenth Century* (Cambridge, MA: MIT Press, 1993).

Davis, Fred, *Yearning for Yesterday: A Sociology of Nostalgia* (New York: Free Press, 1979).

Denning, Michael, *The Cultural Front: The Laboring of American Culture in the Twentieth Century* (London: Verso, 1996).

Derrida, Jacques, *Of Grammatology*, Translated by Gayatri Chakravorty Spivak (Baltimore: Johns Hopkins University Press, 1976).

Douglass, Frederick, *Narrative of the Life of Frederick Douglass: An American Slave Written by Himself* ([1845] New York: Signet, 1968).

Du Bois, W. E. B., *The Souls of Black Folk* ([1903] New York: Dover, 1994).

Evans, Walker, *Walker Evans at Work* (London: Thames and Hudson, 1984).

———, *American Photographs* (New York: Doubleday, 1938).

Fabien, Johannes, *Time and the Other: How Anthropology Makes Its Object* (New York: Columbia University Press, 1983).

Faulkner, William, *As I Lay Dying* (New York: Vintage, 1964).

Felreis, Alan, *Modernism from Right to Left: Wallace Stevens, the Thirties and Literary Radicalism* (Cambridge: Cambridge University Press, 1994).

Freud, Sigmund, *Civilization and Its Discontents* ([1930] New York: Norton, 1989).

Glassie, Henry, *Folk Housing in Middle Virginia* (Knoxville: University of Tennessee Press, 1975).

Goldberg, Vicky, *Photography in Print: Writings from 1816 to the Present* (Albuquerque: University of New Mexico Press, 1982).

Gorman, Paul, *Left Intellectuals and Popular Culture in Twentieth-Century America* (Chapel Hill: University of North Carolina Press, 1996).

Hegeman, Susan, *Patterns for America: Modernism and the Concept of Culture* (Princeton, NJ: Princeton University Press, 1999).

Horney, Karen, *The Neurotic Personality of Our Time* ([1937] New York: Norton, 1964).

Huyssen, Andreas, *After the Great Divide: Modernism, Mass Culture, Postmodernism* (Bloomington: Indiana University Press, 1986).

*I'll Take My Stand: The South and the Agrarian Tradition*, 12 Southern Writers ([1930] Louisiana: Library of Southern Civilization, 1977).

Kammen, Michael, *Mystic Chords of Memory: The Transformation of Tradition in American Culture* (New York: Knopf, 1991).

Kazin, Alfred, *On Native Grounds: An Interpretation of Modern American Prose Literature* (New York: Reynal and Hitchcock, 1942).

Kidd, Stuart, *Farm Security Administration Photography, the Rural South, and the Dynamics of Image-Making, 1935–1943* (New York: Edwin Mellen Press, 2004).

Korzybski, Alfred, *Science and Sanity: An Introduction to Non-Aristotelian Systems and General Semantics* (Lakeville, CT: International Non-Aristotelian Library, 1933).

Lofaro, Michael A. and Hugh Davis, editors, *James Agee Rediscovered: The Journals of* Let Us Now Praise Famous Men *and Other New Manuscripts* (Knoxville: University of Tennessee Press, 2005).

Madden, David, and Jeffrey J.Folks, *Remembering James Agee* (Athens: University of Georgia Press, 1997).

Mitchell, W. J. T., *Iconology: Image, Text, Ideology* (Chicago: Chicago University Press, 1986).

*Movies and Methods* Vol. 1, edited by Bill Nichols (Berkeley: University of California Press, 1976).

Mumford, Lewis, *Interpretations and Forecasts: 1922–1972* (New York: Harcourt, Brace, 1979).

Nichols, Bill, *Representing Reality* (Bloomington: Indiana University Press, 1991).

Olney, James, *Autobiography: Essays Theoretical and Critical* (Princeton, NJ: Princeton University Press, 1980).

———, *Metaphors of Self: The Meaning of Autobiography* (Princeton, NJ: Princeton University Press, 1972).

Orwell, Miles, *The Real Thing: Imitation and Authenticity in American Culture, 1880–1940* (Chapel Hill and London: University of North Carolina Press, 1989).

*The Oxford English Dictionary* (London: Oxford University Press, 1961).

Peeler, David, *Hope Among Us Yet: Social Criticism and Social Solace in Depression America* (Athens: Georgia University Press, 1987).

Pells, Richard H., *Radical Visions and American Dreams: Culture and Social Thought in the Depression Years* (New York: Harper and Row, 1973).

Perloff, Marjory, *The Futurist Movement: Avant-Garde, Avant-Guerre, and the Language of Rupture* (Chicago: University of Chicago Press, 1986).

Pound, Ezra, *ABC of Reading* ([1934] London: New Directions, 1987).

———, *Machine Art and Other Writings: The Lost Thought of the Italian Years*, edited and introduced by Maria Luisa Ardizzone (Durham, NC: Duke University Press, 1996).

Rabinowitz, Paula, *They Must Be Represented* (London: Verso, 1994).

Rasula, Jed, and Steve McCaffery, editors, *Imagining Language: An Anthology* (Cambridge, MA: MIT Press, 1998).

Richards, I. A., *How to Read a Page: A Course in Effective Reading with an Introduction to a Hundred Great Words* (London: Routledge, 1961).

Ruby, Jay, *A Crack in the Mirror: Reflexive Perspectives in Anthropology* (Philadelphia: University of Pennsylvania Press, 1982).

Schlesinger, Arthur M., *The Age of Roosevelt: The Politics of Upheaval* (Boston: Houghton Mifflin, 1960).

Southall, Thomas W., *Of Time and Place: Walker Evans and William Christenberry* (San Francisco: Friends of Photography, 1990).

Spiegel, Alan, *James Agee and the Legend of Himself* (Columbia: University of Missouri Press, 1998).

Staub, Michael E., *Voices of Persuasion: The Politics of Representation in 1930s America* (Cambridge: Cambridge University Press, 1994).

Stott, William, *Documentary Expression and Thirties America* (Chicago: University of Chicago Press, 1973).

Szalay, Michael, *New Deal Modernism: American Literature and the Invention of the Welfare State* (Durham, NC: Duke University Press, 2000).

Taylor, Gordon O., *Chapters of Experience: Studies in Twentieth Century American Autobiography* (New York: St. Martin's Press, 1983).

Trachtenberg, Alan, *Reading American Photographs: Images as History, Mathew Brady to Walker Evans* (New York: Hill and Wang, 1989).

Turner, Victor, *Dramas, Fields, and Metaphors: Symbolic Action in Human Society* (Ithaca, NY: Cornell University Press, 1974).

Welty, Eudora, *On Writing* (New York: Random House, Modern Library Edition, 2002).

West, Nancy, *Kodak and the Lens of Nostalgia* (Charlottesville: Virginia University Press, 2000).

White, John, *Literary Futurism: Aspects of the First Avant-Garde* (Oxford: Clarendon Press, 1990).

Woolley, Edwin C., *The Mechanics of Writing: A Compendium of Rules regarding Manuscript-Arrangement, Spelling, the Compounding of Words, Abbreviations, the Representation of Numbers, Syllabication, the Use of Capitals, the Use of Italics, Punctuation, and Paragraphing* (Boston: D. C. Heath,1909).

Wright, Richard, with photo direction by Edward Rosskam, *12 Million Black Voices* ([1941] New York: Thunder's Mouth Press, 2002).

# CONTRIBUTORS

**Caroline Blinder** is lecturer in American Literature at Goldsmiths, University of London. She has previously published *A Self-Made Surrealist: Ideology and Aesthetics in the Work of Henry Miller* (2000), "The Transparent Eyeball: Emerson and Walker Evans" Mosaic, 2004, "Another Kind of Patriotism: Robert Frank's *The Americans*" in *Photography and Literature* (2005), "Looking for Love in All the Wrong Places: Brassaï's Photographs in André Breton's *Mad Love*," History of Photography (2005), "The Bachelor's Drawer: Art and Artefact in the Work of Wright Morris" in *Writing with Light: Words and Photographs in American Texts*, ed. Mick Gidley (2009), "Not so Innocent: Vision and Culpability in Weegee's Photographs of Children" in *Photographs, Histories, and Meanings* (2009) "Articulating the Depression: *You Have Seen Their Faces* and *American Exodus*" in *The Photobook from Talbot to Rucha and Beyond* (2010).

**Sue Currell** is senior lecturer in American Literature at the University of Sussex. She is author of *the March of Spare Time: The Problem and Promise of Leisure During the 1930s* (2005), "Streamlining the Eye: Speed Reading and the Revolution of Words, 1870–1940" in *Residual Media* ed. Charles Acland (2005), "Depression and Recovery: Self-Help and America in the Great Depression," in *Historicizing Lifestyle*, ed. David Bell and Joanne Hollows and "The New Deal for Leisure: Federal Recreation Programs During the Great Depression" in *Loisir et Liberté en Amerique du Nord* (2008). Her books also include *American Culture in the 1920s* (2009) and *Popular Eugenics: National Efficiency and American Mass Culture in the 1930s* (2006).

**John Dorst** specializes in the ethnographic investigation of contemporary vernacular life, material culture, and ethnographic theory. His major publications are *The Written Suburb: An American Site, an Ethnographic Dilemma*, a "postmodern" ethnography of an elite suburb, *Looking West* (1989), an examination of visual discourses in the contemporary American West, *Looking West* (1999) and "Rereading Mules and Men: Towards the Death of the Ethnographer" in Cultural Anthropology (2009) . He has been a Fulbright Senior Fellow at the Roskilde University Center in Denmark. With the assistance of a Guggenheim Fellowship, he is currently working on an ethnographic study of the production and display of animal artifacts.

**Mick Gidley** is emeritus professor at Leeds University. His books include *American Photography* (1983), and, as editor or coeditor, *Views of American Landscapes* (1989), *Locating the Shakers* (1990), *Representing Others: White Views of Indigenous Peoples* (1992), *Modern American Culture* (1993), *American Photographs in Europe* (1994), and *Modern American Landscapes* (1995). His recent books are *Edward S. Curtis and the North American Indian Project in the Field* (2003); *Photography and the USA* (2010) and, as editor, *Views of American Landscapes* (1989, 2007) and *Writing with Light: Words and Photographs in American Texts* (2009).

**Paul Hansom** is lecturer in English at Ithaca College and a resident faculty member at the Frederick Douglass Academy in Harlem. His books include *Twentieth Century European Cultural Theorists* (2001) and *Twentieth Century American Cultural Theorists* (2004) part of the Dictionary of Literary Biography series and an anthology on the intersections between modernist aesthetics and twentieth-century Photography: *Literary Modernism and Photography* (2002).

**Paula Rabinowitz** is professor of English and Samuel Russell Chair in the Humanities at the University of Minnesota. She has written, among other works, "Social Representations within American Modernism," *Cambridge Companion to American Modernism*. Ed. Walter Kalaidjian (2005), "*Alfred Stieglitz and Georgia O'Keeffe on the Thirtieth Floor*" in *Public Space, Private Lives: Race, Gender, Class, and Citizenship in New York, 1890–1929* (2004). Her books include, *Labour and Desire: Women's Revolutionary Fiction in Depression America* (1991), *They Must be Represented: The Politics of Documentary* (1994), and *Black, White and Noir* (2002). She also coedited: *Writing Red: An Anthology of American Women Writers 1930–1940* (1991).

**William Stott's** *Documentary Expression and Thirties America* (1973) remains one of the seminal texts on documentary writing and a classic of American cultural history. After receiving his PhD at Yale University, he held a Guggenheim fellowship and was later a Fulbright lecturer in London. He is the coauthor of *On Broadway: Performance photographs by Fred Fehl*. After teaching documentary studies for many years at the University of Texas at Austin, Prof. Stott's *Write to the Point and Feel better about Your Writing* was published in 1984.

**Alan Trachtenberg** is professor emeritus of English and American Studies at Yale University. Trachtenberg's books include *The Incorporation of America: Culture and Society in the Gilded Age* (1982), *Brooklyn Bridge: Fact and Symbol* (1965), *Reading American Photographs: Images as History, Mathew Brady to Evans Walker* (1989), *Shades of Hiawatha: Staging Indians, Making Americans, 1890–1930* (2004). A volume of his selected essays, *Lincoln's Smile & Other Enigmas*, appeared in 2007, along with the twenty-fifth Anniversary Edition of *The Incorporation of America*. His current projects include a study of photographs and fictions by Wright Morris, and a study of the first edition (1855) of Walt Whitman's *Leaves of Grass*.

# INDEX

CONCORDIA UNIVERSITY LIBRARIES
MONTREAL